A Drop of Mercy

A novel by

Betzy Miesen

A Drop of Mercy

By Betzy Miesen

This is a work of fiction. Names, characters, places, and incidents either are the byproduct of the author's imagination or are used fictionally. Any resemblance to actual persons, living or dead, or locales is entirely coincidental.

Books by the same author

A.M.O. Junko and the Prophesy.

Acknowledgements

Cinny Green

Table of Contents

Chapter 1
Little Sister, Little Aunt

As I was sweeping the uneven floor of my porch, I blew a lock of damp black hair from my face. It was afternoon, and the sun was about to set on the horizon, its hazy, warm colors lightly caressing anything it touched. The old fan was thankfully circulating the hot Panamanian air in the otherwise stuffy house. An unexpected breeze stirred the sheer curtains ever so slightly. Dust rose up from the old rug, but I wouldn't hit it outside that day. It was a job for the next.

There were too many things for me to do. I still had to finish dinner and clean the furniture. Thankfully, there wasn't much to clean. I had a faded yellow couch that in some places had only a few threads holding the fabric together, which I often took to my neighbor to fix. I could manage to take it outside and hit it with a stick to get all the accumulated dirt and grit out. Then I usually washed it by hand, but that would have to wait too. I wished that days like today were thirty hours long instead of only twenty-four, so I could take a long nap. Raising three kids on my own, I hardly had time to sleep a full six hours at night. I could not have managed without my mom's help. I was so glad—and fortunate—that she lived with me.

"Lluvia, I think the beans need more water. They're still hard. It will probably be another thirty minutes." My mother Juana grabbed an empty ice cream container and walked toward the outdoor sink in the laundry room. We used everything available to accomplish our endless chores. She moved aside a container full of wet clothes that I was whiting to get ready to hang outside. "Lluvia, you are trying to do so much at once." Mom shouted with her back to me at the sink. "Do you want me to hang these shirts? We have about one full hour of good sun. The kids don't have any clean clothes for school tomorrow. I'll hang up their uniforms." She filled the ice cream container with water and walked slowly inside, careful not to spill on herself. I heard the sizzle as she poured it into the pot of red beans. A few minutes later, she came back out carrying the orange bucket full of clothes. She dropped the bucket on the grass with a thump by the clothesline and quickly clipped on the first school uniform. From where I stood sweeping, Mamita looked like a painting. One of the five white arches that wrapped around the porch outlined her figure like a picture frame. Her hazelnut colored skin and her curly white hair contrasted each other brilliantly. It seemed to me that she was glowing with a celestial light, and she looked like a picture-perfect angel. How lucky I was to have her. She was there for me, unconditionally, from the day she took me in as her own when I was merely eight months old to today, when I had three kids to look after.

My little girl Susana ran across the yard and knocked over the orange bucket. "Go around, Susana, you're getting the clothes dirty." With a sigh, I walked towards the clothesline to help pick up the spilled laundry.

"Stop, Susana!" Juana shouted and threw her hands up in frustration. "Look! She already dirtied a shirt with ash."

"Ash?" I looked at the hem of the hanging shirt and saw the slash of gray on the white cotton.

"Yes, it is." Juana grumbled.

I scanned the yard to find Susana, and there she sat under a tree with three medium stones placed on the ground in front of her in the shape of a triangle. They held a screen that looked like something from her brother Marcelo's chicken pen. A small campfire burned between the stones and nearly fifty *marañon* shells were scattered on the ground haphazardly, blackened by the fire and cracked open to get to the cashews inside.

Susana looked quickly over her shoulder and said, "I'm sorry, Mamita. I'll wash it again."

I wasn't convinced. I tossed the ashy shirt over the clothesline and walked toward the marañon tree to see what she was up to. Susana was too busy to notice me coming. Her long black hair looked nearly red in the afternoon sun, and her young tan face was completely covered in dirt. Her white summer dress wasn't white anymore.

"How in the world could you get so many cashews from so little fruit?" There were only about twenty marañon apples discarded near her, but she had over fifty nuts still roasting on the makeshift grill.

She jumped up. "I need more! I have a friend coming for dinner" Under a large branch of the marañon tree, she stepped on a stick with her bare feet. "Ow!" She whined and bounced up and down.

"Why aren't you wearing your shoes, Susana?" I asked in exasperation.

She looked at me as if the answer was obvious. "I don't want to get them dirty." She quickly forgot about the stick stabbing her foot and reached for more apples. "Like I said, I have a friend coming for dinner."

The nuts of the marañon were attached to the bottom of the apple-like fruit hanging on the tree. After clutching the fruit, she twisted the shells off and threw the rest away carelessly. The yard was full of red marañon pulp. Fortunately, she wasn't interested in the fruit. Its juice can permanently stain clothes. Not that I was worried about her formerly white-now-grey-and-black dress. I knew it would take many days in the bucket to turn it back to white, because ash really sticks to clothes.

She placed the shells in the hem of her dress, creating a basket out of the fabric, and carried them back to the fire pit. Susana laid them out into little rows. She would roast them next, then crack them open, discard the shell, and throw the nuts into a glass milk jar. I had taught her how to do all this when she was a toddler.

"I took some from the branches." Susana gestured toward the tree without taking her hands off the shells.

I looked up at the branches, noting that the lower branches were sparsely populated with fruit, while the upper branches still had a lot.

"I am glad you're only four feet tall or the whole tree would be empty." I smiled. "Your father would find it funny if he got to see how you assault the tree." I always talked to her about her father even though she had never met him—or seemed to care all that much. I suppose it was more for me than her.

Without acknowledging the mention of her father, Susana triumphantly stated, "I also got a bunch of cashews from Adan and Tino. We were gambling and I won!" She moved her hair out of her face while roasting the nuts, smudging even more ash on her cheek.

I crossed my arms sternly. "Gambling?" But I was curious too.

"Yes, all the kids in the neighborhood do it." She continued to poke her harvest over the fire.

"How do you guys play this game?"

"See that hole?" she asked. It was a deep one underneath another tree in the backyard, a sprawling oak. The hole was nestled comfortably between two roots.

I smiled softly. "Yes, of course. You know, your father, Walter, dug that, for some reason or other." Funny, I thought, he left so many years ago, but it seems so recent. We're still technically married; he didn't want the hassle of a divorce. Yes, that was Walter.

Ignoring me, Susana continued explaining the rules of the game as she cracked open charred shells with a stone. "I bet as many cashews as I want, like twenty. Then, my friends will have to bet the same amount. If they're running out of seeds, they have to share with someone else so they can match my bet."

She filled the milk jar up with cashews, grabbed another container made of a paper carton cut in half, and proceeded to fill up that one as well. "Then, because I won before," she continued, "it was my turn again. I got forty seeds with my two hands. I stay about ten feet away, I aim it towards the hole and throw it inside. If I call pairs and the seeds that got in are in pairs, I win. If I call odds and they're not odd, I lose."

"How could you hold forty seeds with your tiny hands?"

She rolled her eyes. "Trust me, I can."

I ignored her offended tone. "What friend is coming?

"She is my aunt. I met her yesterday. She said that she's your little sister."

"My what?" I was confused, but also kind of amused because I enjoyed her active story-telling imagination. "Tell me about her."

"Her name is Xiomara."

I sat down, began to crack and sort the seeds, too, and asked, "How did you two meet?"

"Well," she said, "I was playing by my school with my friends, and she just walked up to me and said, 'Your mom is my older sister. You have to call me Aunt Xiomara.' Of course, I didn't believe her. She's black and she's eight years old. But then this lady crossed the street to join the conversation and said it was true."

Heat rose inside me as I realized that the story Susana was telling might not be a product of her imagination. I knew that Juana was not my biological mother, but this was too crazy to believe. Tentatively, with my heart thumping out of my chest, I asked her, "Did the lady tell you her name?"

Susana nodded and said, "Oh, yeah. She said her name was Elisa."

My heart dropped, and my stomach turned to lead.

"Susana!" a girl shouted across the unpaved street, waving her arms frantically to get my daughter's attention.

"There she is!" Susana ran with bare feet to meet her. She hopped over the puddle of water created by this morning's rain and nimbly danced around debris lying on the ground.

I returned to my porch and leaned on the broom in the doorway. I suddenly felt very dizzy. Flashbacks assaulted me: A young woman with frown lines marring her otherwise beautiful face. Crying and kicking and screaming.

Mamita finished hanging the kids' uniforms and I went to the kitchen. As I stirred the beans I felt like I was drowning in memories of the past. Looking out the window, I could see the girl Xiomara more clearly. Her dress was a gorgeous orange color that contrasted with her dark skin. She seemed to be well cared for. Her dress looked expensive and her hair was combed and braided back. Her shoes were sparkling white, unusual in this neighborhood of Panama City; everywhere you looked there was mud and dirt. The girls were giggling as they walked up on the porch.

"Xiomara, what took you so long? Dinner's almost done." Susana asked playfully. "Come on, I want you to meet my mom … or, your sister. That's weird!"

Susana ran into the kitchen. Xiomara paused at the doorway, straightening the hem of her dress nervously. "C'mon!" Susana pulled her new friend's hand.

"Are you sure?" Xiomara's eyes darted back and forth from Susanna to me. "I don't know if she'll like me. Our mom said they haven't seen each other in *years*."

As they stood in front of me, I saw their eyes burning with curiosity about how we could be separated for so long without seeing or hearing each other. To be fair, I wasn't quite sure myself. I was feeling a whirlwind of emotions: confusion, anger, grief, joy, and sadness, all clawing each other and fighting each other to be the dominant one. I swallowed hard. "Dinner's not quite ready. Come, girls, roast us more marañones." I led them to the porch and sent them out to the yard.

I watched them play together like instant best friends, and then I looked away and continued sweeping the floor. The woman who raised me, Juana, my *real mother*, came out of the kitchen.

"Who is that with Susana? A new friend?"

I couldn't look at her and felt tears burn the corner of my eyes. "She is Elisa's youngest daughter." I swept harder, as though I could sweep away my fears and bottled-up anger.

Mom smiled gently, touched my arm, and said, "If you sweep the floor any harder, you'll make a hole in the floor."

Suddenly I just couldn't hold back, and hot tears flowed down my cheeks. "Why haven't I just had a normal life?" Juana walked toward me and reached out to give me a hug. "Why wasn't I worthy of her, Mamita? How could she just … just cast me out of her life like I was trash when she didn't get what she wanted? And then she had the nerve to come back to the city and raise four other kids, and not once come to see me? Just like when I was a baby."

"She was young, Lluvia."

"That is no excuse!" I hissed, broke away from her and leaned on one of the pillars, feeling like I was collapsing into myself. "I had three kids on my own, a single mother. I raised them by myself with only you to help me. I had Omar when I was seventeen, but you didn't see me abandoning him! Walter left. He didn't take me seriously, or Panama, or the kids. Panama isn't like Pennsylvania. It isn't 'America the Great.' None of this was permanent for him. He was always going to leave. I never thought about going after him, or leaving my children. *Never, Juana.*" I only ever called her by her first name when I was seething, but she knew that it wasn't directed at her, so she took it in stride.

"He did ask you to leave with him to the United States."

"Yes, but I couldn't leave you behind, Juana. You're family too."

She took both my hands in hers, just like she used to when I was little and upset. Her hands always gave me comfort, and throughout the years they had grown firmer and aged, just like the rest of her. I smiled at the gesture in spite of my anger.

"Come here. Let's sit down. Have a break." She laughed. "We haven't been able to sit all day."

We sat in the chairs on the porch. The girls tended the cashews. A breeze blew enough to keep us cool.

"Do you know what it's like to know that your mother lives just blocks away and won't even say something as simple as hi?" I wrapped my arms around my waist, trying to comfort myself.

"Yes, dear, I was there with you." Juana paused. "Lluvia, you have to understand that your mother had it very hard. She was young, very young, only fourteen when she came to the city for the first time."

I sighed. "This is the same old story that ..."

"Yes, but every time we hear a story we catch a piece of it we didn't hear the first time ... or the tenth time. So I am going to tell you again." And Juana continued as if I had never heard it before. "Elisa's family lived in the Province of Darién, in a small village in a jungle cut off from the rest of the world. They are called the Chocó people and they ate what they hunted or grew in small gardens. The only medicines were wild herbs prepared by healers. Men and women made decisions together, not with leaders. Although there were no shops, no grocery markets, little money, few cars, bad roads, most were content with that life and still are today. Only a trusted few came to the city in boats to exchange crops, carvings, and their amazing baskets for clothes and other things ... oh-oh, the beans."

Juana jumped up to check the pot and add water. She slipped back onto her chair and dropped a little basket on my lap. I shifted restlessly but picked it up and felt the gentle shape. I remembered the colorful blossoms along the edge and the circle design in the center. I looked again.

Juana pointed at the bottom. The circle was actually a turtle shape. "That turtle was your grandmother's signature. Flor was a fine basket maker before she disappeared on a trip into the jungle to get strips of chunga palm. Elisa's father, your grandfather Yobani went to find her and he never returned either."

"Okay," I said grudgingly as I traced the turtle with my finger. I was seeing something new. Juana was always at least partly right. I was curious but I still hoped I would never see my mother's jungle home just two hundred miles south of Panama City ... or her. Unfortunately, now I might have to.

Mamita continued. "Elisa was raised by her aunt Ninfa. She was smart and curious. Perhaps because she had no parents ... who knows why ... she always wanted to go with the traders and do business for her village in La Palma on the coast and beyond, but she was never chosen—until she was fourteen. One day, one of the designated traders, an elder woman, got sick and somebody needed to replace her because everything was already arranged. Bags were full, baskets woven for sale, a truck hired to take the goods and traders over the rough road to the river where canoes awaited. Elisa was chosen to go with Jito. Knowing Elisa didn't want to come back, Ninfa gave her this basket as a keepsake and reminder that she always had a home in Setegantí."

Chapter 2
Seteganti
1948

Elisa sat next to her Aunt Ninfa at the meeting in the *tambo*. The people had a big problem. "Our plantains, bananas, cassava, yams will spoil. We cannot wait for Marcela to get better," cried out a woman across from her in the circle. She shifted her infant from one breast to another. "I need to trade my maize and cacao. I need cloth; the boys need short pants for the new school. Teacher won't let them come in their thongs."

"And I need a new machete," added an older man with a hoarse voice.

Others called out their needs too: axe-heads, pots and pans, salt.

"And medicine for Marcela!"

Jaibana the healer leaned against a post. "She'll be all right. I have clove vine for her fever."

It was the night before Jito and Marcela, the community's traders, were supposed to leave for La Palma and Panama City. Jito stood up and said, "I can take them on my own."

Jaibana shook his head. "We always do things as a community."

Below the hut on stilts, an old rusted truck was stacked with bags and baskets, loaded and ready to head downstream to the province's capitol, and everyone in the village was at the meeting in the tambo, trying to decide whether they should abandon the trip. Naturally there was an uproar; it was so important to their subsistence. The families all had to agree.

Elisa was nervous. She sat in the middle of the tight circle, and felt the tension as each person tried to voice his or her thoughts on the matter. Yet she knew what she wanted, and she knew it was a long shot. She was too young, only fourteen, and a female on top of that. But Marcela was a woman and she had learned to trade somehow. Elisa held her chin up high, trying her best to appear confident, and even though she felt like her heart would pound out of her head, she spoke up. "I will replace Marcela." The people instantly hushed and, instead of yelling they whispered to each other, although she wasn't quite sure which was worse. Her voice and bravado cracked. "I've helped her take count of the goods before. Aunt Ninfa taught me how to write Spanish and I already made the list of what everyone wants, and I know who to talk to." She started to fiddle with her *paruma*-skirt.

Jaibana pursed his lips, leaned out of the tambo, and called to a woman below. "What about you, Lara? Will you go?"

A woman wearing several seed necklaces was bathing her toddler in a wooden tub below the notched log ladder that led up the stilts into the hut. She scowled, shook her head, and pointed to her child as if that explained it.

Two old men lying down on mats didn't really seem to care either way, since they were drinking chicha from a jug. Another young mother with her infant across her lap seemed to want to say something, but she was cut off by one of the drunk men who said, "I need my tobacco. Just let Elisa go." The traders eyed her up and down, sizing her up, but finally relented with shrugs. Her Aunt Ninfa sighed. Everyone finally looked at Jaibana who stared at her as if he could see into her heart, and then nodded his head and said, "Be ready." Elisa felt joy and relief roll over her in waves, so she climbed down the ladder, and ran to prepare for the next morning. I can't believe it, she thought. I'm going to the city!

It was almost dark. She was unsure what to bring on her first trip away from the village. She knew she couldn't wear traditional clothes that left her bare-chested, so she spread her few town clothes— all gifts from Aunt Ninfa—on top of her mat. Aunt Ninfa helped her pack them into a basket along with some food for the long trip to La Palma and then the boat ride to Panama City.

"This is it." She grabbed the long brown skirt that her Aunt Ninfa had made her. She had traded cacao beans for the cotton cloth. Ninfa was a single mother who had two kids on her own with different dads, and like Elisa, the kids had never even seen their fathers. Her second husband had gone with Elisa's father south into the jungle to hunt for the missing women's chunga-gathering group that had taken Elisa's mother and never returned. Was it a panther that killed them? A swamp? Criminals hiding out in the jungle? They never knew but, in spite of her grief, Ninja had taken in Elisa. That's what families did in their village.

"I still haven't traded you for this skirt," Elisa said nervously.

"Don't worry about it." Ninfa waved it off. "I got some more material coming this week from the baskets you'll trade for me. Business is good. And I just finished an order of dresses for a *quinceañera* party in La Palma ... Those Panamanian families pay a lot for their daughters' fifteenth birthday parties. This skirt is my gift to you for being so bold. And so are these." She pulled out a pair of black semi-boots." Eliza gasped with pleasure. Ninfa chuckled. "No need to wear sandals with that pretty skirt." She hugged Elisa, pulling her in close.

Elisa closed her eyes and breathed in the aroma of the sugar cane Ninfa had been pressing that afternoon. "Thank you, Ninfa. You are more like my sister than an aunt."

"I like how it looks on you. It snugs your figure so beautifully. If you told someone you are fourteen, they would think you are lying."

Elisa smiled. "How old do I look?"

"Easily eighteen. But be smart and watch out for men." Ninfa said with a shake of her head and a wicked grin, and she suddenly grabbed her niece and started yanking playfully on Elisa's ears. "Make sure you hide these funny ears so no boy can see them."

"I don't have funny ears," Elisa said indignantly and pushed Ninfa on the mat. Elisa then jumped on top of her aunt and tickled her. They both giggled uncontrollably for what seemed like forever. Exhausted by laughter, they sat facing each other for a while. An old clock in the corner of the room went *tick-tock, tick-tock, tick-tock.* Everything else in the room was silent.

"Are you sure about this?" Ninfa wasn't joking or light hearted any more. She looked genuinely worried.

Tick-tock, tick, tock.

"Yes, I am sure. I've been waiting for this moment for a long time."

Ninfa gave her a soft smile. "My brave Elisa. You are coming back, right?"

Elisa sat up, tucking her knees under her chin and wrapping her arms around her legs. "To be honest, I don't know yet. I want to know if there's something else besides having babies. Here some girls are pregnant by the time they're twelve. I've seen how hard it is to carry a baby and then care for it. You of all people should know that." Her words carried a sharp edge, and Ninfa went quiet. Elisa's eyes widened as she realized that what she said was horrible. "Oh, Ninfa, you know I didn't mean it like that." She reached for Ninfa's hand, but her aunt shifted it ever so slightly away, enough to let her hand slide back down to her side. "Besides, Jito can bring back the supplies to the village. No one would miss me." Ninfa stared up at the ceiling, obviously trying to will away tears. "Thank God I didn't start my noontime until twelve, because some girls can get pregnant at eight or ten."

Ninfa said nothing.

Tick-tock, tick-tock, tick-tock, tick-tock, tick-tock, tick ...

"I can't believe that old clock still works." Elisa paused. "I want to find a different future for me, Ninfa.

Maybe I can find work, then go to school and be somebody ... I will come and get you and your kids. You will be a great seamstress. You can even own a fancy shop like Jito tells us about."

"I know you will do great, Elisa ... just please be careful. Don't trust anyone. I've heard stories ... city people have another world altogether. They don't watch out for each other. It's dangerous. By the way, I want you to take this with you." She handed Elisa a small basket with colorful flowers decorating the edge and a circular turtle woven into the center. There were several ten Balboa bills folded in the bottom.

"Oh, Ninfa."

"I've saved the money for you for a long time. The basket was your mother's." Elisa held it to her chest with her eyes closed. "Well, I guess it's time for you to rest."

Elisa tucked the basket and money deep into her bundle of travel clothes. "Can you stay with me until I fall asleep?"

"Of course." Together, they shoved everything off the mat, turned the oil lamp off, and each claimed a spot to sleep on. The sound of the night creatures was hypnotizing and grew into a crescendo as the rest of the village sounds died down; although Elisa felt safe perched above the jungle floor, she lay awake in the dark.

Tick-tock, tick-tock, tick, tick ...

The old clock was finally done. Raindrops on the palm leaves took over its beat.

At dawn the rusty truck waited outside the tambo and Elisa jumped in. She sat next to the passenger window in the cab. Smoothing her brown skirt, she grinned at Jito and the driver. "I've never been out of the village. How are we going to get to Panama City?" She looked back at the high stack of goods strapped into the back.

"This truck is going to take us to the dock at Chepigana—not too far but it's a really rough road — and from there we load everything on the *cayuco* and *piragua* dugouts that take us downriver to La Palma in one morning. Tonight, we take a sea-going boat to the Port of Panama."

Elisa looked out the window; her face was sweaty from the heat and humidity. Her black, straight hair stuck to her neck. She fanned her face with a feather fan that Ninfa gave her at the last minute.

"No worries, we're still on time." Jito stared out the front window. "Unless we get stuck. It's been raining all night. It's hard to see the depth of those puddles."

On her left, the driver looked at Elisa's worried face and chuckled. "We'll make it on time. We always do."

"What's your name?"

He grinned shyly. "Bo … short for Bombóra. I'm from Moque." Elisa looked closely at his big eyes and saw that he did truly look like an owl. He slowed down, almost to the point of stopping. "Guys watch out. This pool of water looks deep. The truck might get wet inside … but I'm not worried about that."

"I'm worried that the engine will stop if it gets wet," said Jito.

"Me too." Bo approached the puddle. "Elisa, raise your feet if you don't want to get soaked."

Elisa looked down. The floorboard had holes, big holes in it. The muddy track was visible below her feet.

The old truck gunned through the puddle with a jolt throwing water up into the cab, and Elisa squealed. "My boots!"

"I told you to raise your feet."

She dried her black semi-boots with a *pañuelo*. Then sat back for the ride over the ruts that were barely a road through the jungle. It seemed to go on forever under a humid canopy of palm fronds. The truck's smell of exhaust, old engine, and oil made her feel sick. At least, the windows were open.

"Are you alright, Elisa? You look pale," asked Jito.

"I'm alright." Elisa felt her breakfast rising. She didn't want the others to know so she opened her window. Ahh, I'm getting closer. Hold it, Elisa ... hold it, she whispered silently to herself.

Jito nudged her. "I don't care what you say. You don't look good."

"I think I smell the river."

"You do. This is it!" Bo drove around one final bend and left the canopy behind. Ahead a few stilt houses were spread on either side of the ruts. Some were thatch tambos and some were worn frame houses. Children peered from the high floors and scrambled down the notched log ladders to run beside the vehicle. The road ended at a shore where boatmen stood beside piraquas, the wooden dugouts, and cayucos, wider boats, some already loaded and waiting to head downstream to the province's capitol, La Palma. A few were waiting to be filled with Jito and Eliza's Setangatí goods.

As soon as the truck stopped, Elisa jumped out. The breakfast of fruit and yams rushed out of her mouth.

"Step away from my truck," yelled Bo. "You're puking all over."

She stepped away to safely vomit without getting it onto anyone or anything. It was over fast. Even though the children laughed at her, she wiped her mouth and said, "Ah. I feel better."

Jito grimaced. "I hope you do. You are going to be in that old rocky cayuco in the middle of the Tuira. What did you eat?"

"The usual. I don't think that made me sick. It's just that I've never been in a truck before ... all the turns and the smell."

"Well, whatever it was, I am glad you're better." Jito handed me a jug of water.

A breeze off the Río Tuira felt like medicine. The water tasted cool and good. Bo and Jito unloaded our goods on the ground. There were about ten sacks each of plantains, bananas, cassava, yams, and cacao as well as many different sized baskets to sell in Panama City. Elisa knew from Martha's ledgers that the baskets were sought after by city vendors and brought the village the most money.

"Good luck to both of you!" called Bo, then he jumped in the truck and bumped it noisily back around the bend into the forest canopy. Elisa remembered too late that Ninfa's fan was still on the dashboard.

Three kids approached Jito. "Do you need help?" asked the tallest.

"How much for loading those sacks in the cayucos?" Jito pointed to the pile on the ground.

"Two Balboas each." Their ash-dark skins looked like they spent every day in the sun and river water. They had on shorts, sandals, and they were shirtless.

"Alright." Jito agreed and pulled two coins for each from his pouch

The kids carried the bags one by one. They loaded two piraguas and four cayucos, leaving just enough room for Jito in one and Elisa in the other.

She watched other passengers boarding some of the other dugouts. They seemed like Chocó people, too, uncertain and speaking their own dialect that Elisa couldn't quite understand. Jito gave a lot of attention to the younger women but Elisa was clearly the youngest of all.

Jito dried his sweaty forehead with his handkerchief. Elisa wondered why he wore long pants and a thick long sleeve shirt. It was so hot and humid. The boatmen were all shirtless and wearing shorts like the children. "Nice breeze." said Jito as he grinned and offered her a hand into the unsteady canoe. "I am sure your stomach appreciates that." He added, "Put your feet in the center!" He stood at the edge of the worn board that connected the boat to the shore. Elisa was glad he grabbed her hand because the boat was tipping sideways with the current. She finally got her balance and sat between the bags. It was surprisingly cozy leaning against a bundle of yams low in the middle of the dugout.

The boatman Erito offered her a small cup of green liquid. "This will keep you from getting sick again."

"Is this medicine?"

"It probably is." He laughed. "Anyway, nobody has died from it in the life I have spent on the river ... I give it to all my passengers to keep you calm and happy to be on this *rio magnífico*!"

Elisa drank, grimaced, and swallowed the bitter tea, noticing that other boatmen were offering similar cups to passengers in their canoes.

The boats moved slowly away from shore, one by one, and became a flotilla heading downstream in the robust current. Elisa looked across the broad waterway wondering what would become of her. She thought, Will I have the courage to stay? Or come back, afraid that I couldn't make it? But the water and the sky and the shore were so lovely she forgot to be afraid. Fish jumped between the canoes and she saw a large turtle rise to the surface and watch them pass. It reminded her of her mother's basket, tucked deep in her own basket of clothes. Birds with broad arched wings swooped over the water snatching bugs. She leaned her head back on the bag of yams. She felt relaxed. She had woken up early this morning. Her eyes were heavy so she closed them and let her hands stroke the rough carved sides of the boat. Then it got dark and a three-toed sloth approached her. He was incredibly slow but that made it even more frightening. "Help!" She screamed but nobody heard her. "Help!" The strange animal had green moss all over its fur. It grabbed her arm with big sharp claws. Everyone in the other boats just minded their business as if this was no big deal. "Help!"

"Young woman, young woman," a voice called through the darkness. Elisa opened her eyes. A boatman from another canoe had pulled alongside and reached over to shake her awake.

"Are you alright?" he asked kindly. "You must have had a scary dream."

"Yes, it was," she answered, sheepishly. "A sloth grabbed me."

He chuckled. "Oh, they're not so dangerous."

"I've never liked them. They would climb into our tambo and walk across me at night." Elisa combed her hair with her hand. "How far are we from La Palma?"

"We should be there shortly, about ten minutes." He pointed ahead. "Watch over there. We're coming into the *Golfo de San Miguel* and you'll be able to see the port."

Elisa scanned the broadening horizon. "I can't see it yet."

"Look this way. Do you see the hundreds of palm trees along the shore?"

"Yes, I do. Oh, now I see some houses. They're like our tambos, raised up to keep animals and snakes out."

"Here sometimes the tide or storm waters come all the way up to touch the floors of the houses."

"Oh, I can see the port now!"

She sat up excitedly, looking from boat to boat for Jito. His canoe was the first to land. In a few minutes, every cayuco and piragua beached near the bigger docks, and the boatmen and passengers congregated on shore. Locals gathered around to help unload. She saw Jito surrounded by a group of women. As she walked quietly over, she could hear snatches of the conversation.

"… not to mention the hotels in Panama that I own. I'm planning to put them up for sale, so I am going to meet up with my agents," said Jito, the big man. She realized now that he wore his long pants and shirt so he wouldn't look like just another Chocó boatman. He'd look like an important trader.

She shook her head at the women who seemed so impressed by this man who just a week ago was hunting wild pigs in the jungle wearing nothing but a thong. She passed by Jito and waited for the boys to unload the cayucos. The houses by the docks looked like something out of a photograph she had once seen back in the village. The colors, oh, the colors were incredible. There were pinks and greens and blues of all shades, brighter than flowers, and they all managed to fit so well with each other. There were also many little fishing boats tied to the docks as well as a larger passenger ferry. The water was a deep blue, the gulf more like she had imagined an ocean would be. Calm waters added to the serene view. She looked up and saw a thick wire strung above the rooftops from one pole to another above the street. Elisa asked a woman near her what they were for. "Lights." The woman smiled at her. "For a few houses."

There were kids playing underneath the houses, laughing and screaming happily, a couple cooked outdoors, their arms wrapped around each other's waist. She saw a black pot with flames dancing underneath it. It took Elisa a moment to realize that there was an elderly woman stirring something in it. She was so tiny and her dress matched the pot.

It was at that moment that Elisa fell in love for the first time, and it was with the new world in front of her, so much bigger than Seteganti and the Chocó life. "Panama, she said softly.

"Almost," Jito grabbed her arm by surprise and said, "Let's go up into town and get a car.

"Where are we going?" Elisa asked incredulously. "You said we can't go to Panama City by road. Where are our goods?"

"Don't worry. They're being loaded on the tugboat that will take us to Panama City overnight. This is how we do it every time." They walked up a short hill and turned onto the main street of La Palma. It was full of small shops serving grilled meat and juices, sellers laid out many small goods from tools to toys on mats in the street. There were only two small cars parked to the side. Elisa thought they were beautifully sleek, and the drivers leaned on them smoking cigarettes. Jito stopped at a red one with some paint scraped off the sides.

"My cousin! How is it going, Abelardo?" Jito called with a cheesy grin pasted on his face.

Abelardo had glassy eyes and a slovenly posture. Elisa smelled chicha. "Same old ... same old. Just living." Jito's cousin slurred his words and chuckled, "Who is the pretty girl?"

"My new trader partner from the village. Learning the ropes."

Abelardo suddenly sobered up, suspicious. "Oh, I know, I know what you're doing," he said, shaking a finger at Jito, which made Elisa grin because seeing Jito get chewed out was always funny to her. Jito had been big-headed since he was able to walk.

Jito spread his arms wide, looking offended. "What do you mean? What am I doing?"

"You, dear cousin, are trying to score a free ride from me."

"I would never ..."

"Look, I know we're family, but you need to pay me. I've got mouths to feed, you know."

"Fine." Jito looked exasperated and defeated. "I'll pay you when we get in the car."

The cousin nodded, "You better or I won't turn the key." He opened the door and held it, gesturing for them to get in. He kind of looked like Jito, from the dark skin to the crook in his nose. The only difference was Jito's hair was close-cut while his cousin's was long, greasy, and scraggly. They got into the taxi, but not before Elisa flashed the cousin a smile. Might as well make a friend of this fellow who stood up to Jito. He grinned back.

Turning to Jito, with a cross look on her face, she said, "I am still confused. Where are we even going?"

"To Las Mercedes?" asked Abelardo. He held his hand out over the seat. "Three balboas."

Jito turned away from her and nodded. He paid the fare.

She tapped his shoulder. "Las Mercedes? Where is that? Why are we going to Las Mercedes?"

"Not far. I have some business to attend to there." He looked out the window.

She felt disappointed. And angry. "Are you dealing with your personal business with *my* village's money?" She said it with viper venom, glaring at him with all her might. He didn't even flinch. "Who knows about this?"

"Listen, kid." Jito finally glared at her directly and made his voice low and forceful, which scared Elisa half to death. "You don't get to judge what I do or choose not to do. You're a kid, you don't even know what's right or wrong in this world. It's not a village where everyone does the same thing forever." He looked out the window again. "You have been nothing but trouble. Throwing up all over the place, then your crazy dream on the boat." He shook his head. "Marcela a least left me alone. I'm going to make sure you don't become a Setegantí trader."

Fear struck Elisa's heart, and she let it slip over her face. Jito glanced at her, and while he didn't say anything, she saw the look of triumph in his eyes.

Abelardo looked in the rearview mirror at his cousin in utter disrespect. She almost cried but, determined not to let Jito see how she felt, she lifted her head and turned away. She waved to three children running next to the car. They were almost as fast as the car plodding over the potholed road. Elisa pretended she didn't see.

After a few twists and turns through the houses of La Palma, Abelardo stopped the car in front of a tiny green wooden shack with a porch. "Here we are."

"You are a good man, cousin," said Jito. "Take care of the family." He handed him five balboas. "Keep this for the return."

"Do I pick you up in two hours as usual?"

"Yes."

On the porch, there was a girl a little older than me. She had beautiful dark curly hair piled on her head and clear olive skin. She was holding a baby that looked like her. "Wait here," Jito ordered. He pointed to a white net hammock tied to two branches of a tree.

Suspicious, she walked to it with her clothes bundle, going around a wet stuffed animal in the grass. It occurred to Elisa that the girl must have at least one other kid. She lay in the hammock as Jito went eagerly into the house with the girl. Elisa felt disgusted and wondered if Yamis, his wife, knew about Jito's little visits to Las Mercedes. She doubted it.

She closed her eyes against the onslaught of anger and mistrust she felt toward Jito. It was then that she realized that she needed to stay in Panama, no matter what. She couldn't go back to that small village of hers with him and his lies when the whole world seemed to be at her fingertips.

I might have enough money from Ninfa to survive for a while in Panama. I will need to get a job, she thought as she sucked on some dried sweet *ciruelo* from her bag. But I am only a child. Who is going to give me a decent job? Doubts hijacked her confidence, leaking in through cracks, oozing down her ribcage, and wrenching her heart.

She lay there for a while, watching one of the neighborhood kids playing fetch with a scruffy black dog. He threw a stick, but the dog looked at him confused, sat down, and watched the little boy, who couldn't have been more than six. The boy threw up his hands, look toward the sky, ran and got the stick, and brought it back to the dog, lecturing the poor thing about the game of fetch. He threw it again, and the dog sat in the same spot, occasionally scratching its ear with its back leg. Elisa, glad for the comic relief, watched them, giggling as the boy retrieved the stick each time.

She heard Abelardo honk his horn, surprised. *Did two hours already pass?* She got out of the hammock and walked to the car, where Abelardo was waiting with the door open, smiling apologetically. "You can get in, kid." She did so, not looking forward to seeing Jito. He closed the door and walked to the other side of the car.

When Jito emerged from the house, the girl's hair was down, and she was only wearing a robe. There was no baby in sight. The boy and the dog ran to the porch.

Abelardo must've seen Elisa's disapproval on her face, because he sighed and said, "Yeah, I hate him for it too."

She turned to him, and said sharply, "Then why do you drive him here?"

He ran a hand over his scraggly hair, not looking her in the eye. "He pays good when he's not trying to get a free ride, and like I said earlier, I've got a family to feed. I wish it were that simple, to just stop driving him, but at what cost?" He sighed again, finally looking her straight in the eye. "Like it or not, he's family."

She turned to look outside the window, watching Jito and the girl, who now looked no older than fifteen, still kissing and smiling on the porch. He was old enough to be her father. Well, maybe not quite.

"Yeah, but that doesn't mean you have to help him be a bad person."

Jito got in the car, buttoning up his shirt and taking a quick glance at Elisa as Jorge started to drive.

I am staying in Panama, she set her decision as she immediately turned to the window, trying to spare herself Jito's hateful glare. She didn't say one word on the way to the port. Not one.

Abelardo dropped them at the dock. "Until next time, primo," he said and gave Elisa a little wink and a smile. "Good luck, girl." It struck her that both Bo and Abelardo had been nice fellows. Not full of themselves like Jito. It was nice to know there were good people outside the village. Jito then led her out to the end of the pier where a big rusty tugboat was tied to the pilings. The boat was called the Doña Flor and was full of trade goods from the Darién province as well as a couple of familiar faces she recognized from the dugouts from Chepigana. Jito shook hands with an old captain who was missing a great many teeth. The man spoke in a foreign language that Elisa could not make out, maybe English, since he said *okay* and *yep* several times, but thankfully Jito responded in Spanish. "Sí, sí, I'm fine with it." Jito motioned for her to come on board the boat. She wanted to know everything since the afternoon at Las Mercedes had taught her to mistrust Jito even more. The more he explained, the more she interrupted and asked her own questions: where were the goods from Seteganti (the captain pointed to the stacks mid ship), when were they leaving (7 pm on the change of tide), how long would it take? The old guy looked baffled by her onslaught of questions so Jito filled in that information. "We'll stop at Chinán to unload their supplies … that town has no roads … and we'll get to Panama City about midnight."

Jito negotiated the price to deliver them all to Panama City. The captain said, "You paid me for the goods. You owe eight balboas for the trip for you and the girl," and Jito handed him ten balboa saying, "Keep the change."

Elisa thought he was being too free with the village resources again, but she since didn't plan to go back and report him, she nodded and turned to nest among their bags again. Suddenly the scent of cooking rice, sofrito, black beans with so many spices bombarded her nose. Overcome with hunger she vaguely registered Jito saying something behind her. "Sorry, what?"

"I asked, are you hungry?"

"Oh, yes, very."

"Come on. Let's get you some good food up on the main street."

With the straps of her own basket of clothes and Ninfa's gift of money safely tucked over her shoulder, they left the dock and wandered back up to the main street of La Palma. It was almost dark, and the vendors were packing up their goods as little restaurants hung lanterns over outdoor tables. Jito walked to a small grey building where a few people sat at tables on a balcony. "This way," he ordered and led her up some stairs on the side of the building. They sat at a table overlooking the bay. Elisa felt exhausted but enchanted by the glimmering lights. A young waiter came and said,

"Tonight we have carnitas and beans or fried sargento and choyote."

Elisa whispered to Jito, "I've never been to a restaurant before. I don't know how to order."

Jito smiled genuinely. Surprisingly. "That's alright. Not many do, the first time." He ordered for them both. "Carnitas and coconut water for the lady. Sargento for me." The waiter nodded and left. Jito spread his arms in a grandiose fashion. "Well, here we are. Halfway to Panama City."

Elisa looked at Jito. He wasn't being terrible like he had been the rest of the trip, in fact he looked rather relaxed. "This place has tasty food."

She decided to cautiously ask him something while he was in a good mood. "How hard it is it to find work in Panama, Jito?"

"Very easy, if you know the right people." He looked at her with a curious grin. "Are you planning to stay?"

She shrugged. "I'm just asking …"

"Look," interrupted Jito, "Panama, can be a dangerous place for a fourteen-year-old girl."

"More than in Darién with snakes and jaguars?"

"Different. Thieves and bad men will take advantage of you. Look, Elisa," Jito held open his hands, "I get it why you came. You want to see something bigger than Seteganti. If you seriously want to stay, I can help you. You're right, Darién can be limiting, mostly because there's no future there. Just the same way of living that our people have done for maybe thousands of years."

The waiter brought their plates of food and she ate with gusto. It was hot and good and the coconut water had been sweetened with plenty of sugar.

He watched her devour her meal. "I know you're ambitious. I actually like that about you. In Panama City maybe you can go to school. Get a trade, like being a seamstress or a shopkeeper or a teacher."

Elisa was uncertain about trusting this man who just a short while ago couldn't wait to get rid of her. Yet he was offering her exactly what she needed: hope.

"Do you want me to help you, or not?" A dull sound startled Elisa from her reverie and Jito's enticing words. She turned around and discovered a small red plastic bottle had fallen from on the floor under a baby at the next table over. The child had short dark curly hair, and his two front teeth were coming in, which she knew because he was grinning at her, his chubby cheeks lifting up and his eyes lighting up. She smiled at him and his family. A blonde man, about ten years younger than the woman, held the child. He picked up the bottle and gave it to the baby, who promptly continued to suck whatever was inside. The lady said a tired thank you in a very thick accent. Elisa did not want to be that woman.

"Elisa!" Jito said under his breath, "I asked do you want help or not? Because I can just take you straight back to Setegantí and ..."

"Yes."

"Yes what?"

"Yes, I want—need—your help."

He straightened his shoulders. "Alright. We'll talk details in Panama City. Let's get back to the boat." He paid for the meal and headed down to the pier and got aboard the Doña Flor. Elisa went straight to the Setegantí bags and curled up, using her own basket as a pillow. She fell into a deep sleep, waking up only briefly in Chinán while the crew unloaded some supplies. The next thing she knew the cargo boat's whistle blew sharp and loud. She jumped up as they navigated through many different sized boats to a dock with a big wooden sign: *El Muelle Fiscal*. Here, Jito was more careful not to take his eyes off their village's goods. He hired a few carts and they followed them into a giant flea market where he negotiated the sale of the food stuffs at one large display. The man bought it all, counted money into Jito's hand. "Twenty, forty, sixty, eighty, one hundred. Again, twenty, forty, sixty, eighty, one hundred. And two twenties and one ten. Two hundred and fifty balboas. Are we good?"

"That is how I calculated it, too." Jito smiled, tucked the bills in his leather pouch, and shook the vendor's hand. "Until next time."

Then he pulled the last cart full of their baskets down a street called *Sal Si Puedes*, or Get Out if You Can. He poked her arm and laughed. "Sure you want to stay?"

She gulped and nodded. She was shocked that so many people were in the streets in the middle of the night, doing business, playing music, eating, laughing. They even passed an alley where a few men were in a fight. She was wide awake with the wonder—and fear—of it.

On Sal Si Puedes, they stepped through a doorway into a courtyard with baskets, blankets, carvings, pottery, and other crafts stacked high against the walls. Elisa recognized these as work from different tribes, some who occasionally came through Seteganti from the Darién jungle.

"May I count the baskets?" asked a woman holding a thick worn notebook with columns of numbers. Jito nodded and she began to scrutinize the workmanship and jot down prices for the different styles and sizes. She even grunted her approval of the ones with exceptional detail. When she was done with her accounting she counted out bills into his hand. Elisa was amazed. The baskets brought three times as much money as all the plantains, cacao, yams, bananas, and other food.

Jito walked next to me down the busy street. "Now it's your turn to do your part young lady ... Do you have your list ready?"

"Yes, I do." Elisa stopped and slipped it out of her bag.

He took her arm. "On now to Calle Abajo, on the #12 bus. Remember that. It will bring you to the market at El

Muelle Fiscal whenever you need to get there … if you need to get back to Chepigana"

The crowded bus smelled unpleasantly like some kind of burned oil. And lots of sweat. When they sat together on a wooden seat, she took a look at the list of items. Back in the village, Marcela had asked her to write down their specific requests. She read them out loud to Jito. "A set of comb, brush, and mirror, a grater, scissors, ten pairs of boys short pants, two metal buckets, three axes, two machetes, ten bars of soap, tobacco, salt, matches, sewing needles, three bolts of blue cotton cloth."

"We are here." Jito grabbed her hand and pulled her off the bus onto a narrow, crowded street. Different kiosks sold their own little trove of treasures.

"Is this Calle Abajo?"

"Yes, it is."

They walked down the street. She smelled incense scents that she later learned to name, that always inspired memories of her first day in Panama City—amber, cedar wood, ginger, and jasmine. Elisa stopped at two kiosks that looked like they had some things on her list.

As she read items to the salesman he began putting twelve of each on the counter. "You get a better deal if you get them by the dozen."

Before she could respond, Jito leaned behind her and said, "You get only what you need. They will try to sell you useless stuff. Trust me, kid, they are good at it. Keep yourself focused. This is Panama."

She purchased exactly one item at a time, slowly but surely getting everything on her list in the right quantity. Despite being lured to buy many other things, I have kept true to my village's needs, she thought proudly. Suddenly she thought about Ninfa for the first time since she had left the Darién, and she missed her deeply. She thought that Ninfa would fit right in on the street of kiosks, making a wonderful business for herself selling children's clothes.

"Okay, Elisa, do you have everything?"

Startled out of her reverie, she replied, "Yes, I do. How will we carry them around?"

"I've got another cart outside. It is time to get a hotel room. I think a storm is coming."

They walked one block and turned into a doorway with a sign over it that said El Sol Hotel, but it looked more like mud than a sun to Elisa. Just as it began to rain, they pulled the small cart into the lobby. "Do you need help with that?" asked the front desk clerk.

"You have a lockup as I remember," said Jito.

"Yep, back here." Jito rolled the goods down the hall and returned with a big key. They paid for two rooms.

"Take these stairs up and make a left on the second floor. Your rooms are 201 and 203."

Elisa was so tired she could hardly get up the stairs. Jito offered to carry her bag for her, she still didn't trust him enough to hand him her meager worldly possessions and the Ninfa's balboas that would get her through her first days alone in Panama City.

The light in the hall was dim and she couldn't read the numbers on the door.

"Here is 201, yours. I'll be next to it if you need me." Jito opened the door for her and then handed her an orange oval key holder.

"I'm getting up early to get the first boat back to La Palma. I'll wake you up for some breakfast, Rest well. I'll see you tomorrow."

He closed the door behind him. She opened the curtain because she didn't yet know about the electric light switch. There was a street light outside the window. Wind slapped rain against the glass. She looked around the room in awe, wondering how a room could be this big and only for one person. She had never had a room to herself before. Not to mention one as scrubbed clean as this one. The bed was neatly done with a green blanket that matched the palm leaves pattern on the pillows. She sat down at the edge of her mattress, pulling her knees up under her chin. Alone completely for the first time ever, she was suddenly overcome with confusion. The beautiful room blurred. "What do I do?" she whispered, her sob muffled by the fabric of her brown skirt. She didn't want to ask the Embera spirits for help since she was leaving them behind. Though she had only been to a few services at the little church in Seteganti —Ninfa didn't think much of the skinny white priest in his dark robe—she looked up toward the ceiling and thought she'd give it a try. "Help me, God, what do I do?"

The tears flowed freely down her amber cheeks as she looked up to what she thought were the heavens. "I'm scared, Lord, and I don't know what to do. All of my life I have been in one place, Seteganti, and even though it is dangerous in its way, it's *safer* than this strange city. It's all I've ever known, but... but I want more. Just ... give me a sign. The priest said if I ask you will come. Help me make a decision. Please."

Nothing happened so Elisa took her semi-boots off and, without bothering to get in her nightgown, crawled under the palm tree patterned covers. She tried again. "God, help me."

She closed her eyes. It wasn't long before she heard someone calling her name.

"Elisa."

It was a breathy, barely-there call, but it made the hair on the back of her neck stand at attention. She slowly sat up, cautious and terrified.

"Hello, who's there? Jito, is it you?"

"Elisa."

There it was again, the same, breathy but louder, more demanding, more... angry.

"Jito, stop it, you're scaring me." But even as she spoke those words, she knew it wasn't him. She doubted it was even human.

"Elisa."

She could feel its dank, rotted breath on her cheek.

She screamed loud and without abandon. The room was suddenly not as beautiful as earlier, the wallpaper was peeling from the walls, the color slowly leeching out of it and into the shadow at the edge of the room, slowly taking form into a tall, demented, impossible figure, dark except for that wicked smile, a smile that gripped her and made her heart freeze, a smile that made her scream die in her throat, a smile that was chillingly white and purely evil, a smile that paralyzed her with fear and fear alone, a smile that made her wish she had never left Chepigana, a smile that …

"ELISA!"

Elisa snapped awake, absolutely terrified and drenched in sweat (or tears).

"ELISA!"

Now she knew it was Jito was banging on the door. She pushed her damp hair back, got up, stumbled across the room in the dark, and opened the door to Jito's incessant knocking.

"What, Jito?" she snapped.

Jito flipped on a switch by the door and the room became bathed in light. Elisa looked at it with stunned wonder.

He looked shocked at her appearance, which was pale and half-crazed, but quickly collected himself. "You were screaming, I wanted to make sure you were okay."

She scoffed with false bravery. "Yeah, well you never bothered to make sure I was okay before. Look, it was just a nightmare, I'm fine. Now, leave me alone."

"A nightmare about what?"

She pushed him out, slammed the door, and crawled back into bed, leaving the bright bare light on. She watched a small clock in the corner, puzzled by the fact that it made no noise when the second hand moved. No tick-tock.

Chapter 3
Panama City

Elisa heard three knocks on the door after her restless night. She sighed and got up, opening the door a crack. It was Jito, but he had changed his clothes and showered.

"It's me Jito."

She opened the door, running her hand through her knotted hair.

Jito took in a sharp breath. "God, Elisa, you look terrible."

She didn't doubt it. She hadn't slept at all since her nightmare, and she probably smelled stale since she wore her travel clothes to bed. She sighed.

"You haven't even showered. It's 5:30, we need to get going soon."

"I know, Jito. I'm coming in a minute."

She moved to close the door, but Jito kept it open with his hand jammed between the door and the wall. "About the conversation we had yesterday ..." Jito put his suitcase down.

"Are you sure you want to go through with this?" he asked, watching her carefully. "I won't be there holding your hand, and, again, Panama is a dangerous place."

"I don't need you to hold my hand. At all. And yes, I'm sure. Chepigana just isn't for me, and I don't want to live there for the rest of my life. I'll take the risk."

Jito stared at her a moment, rolled his eyes wondering why she was the way she was, and reached for a pen and paper in his bag. He scribbled something down.

"Here, this is my sister Prudencia's phone number and her address."

Elisa looked at him curiously. "I didn't know you had a sister here. I thought your three sisters were in Chepegani."

"Different father."

"Oh, I guess that's how you learned to be such a ..."

"Drop it if you still want me to help." He scowled at her. She thought he didn't look like he'd slept too well himself. She held her hand up in a kind of surrender. "Okay. I already told Prudencia about you. There's a pay phone at the corner. Tell her you are coming and then take the bus that says Concepción - Juan Diaz or catch a taxi, a yellow car that has *T-A-X-I* written on the side."

She took the piece of paper and folded it into a tiny square. "I've heard about phones but never used one."

"You can read the dial. It's easy. Put the coin in the slot and listen for the tone. Then dial these numbers. You're determined and stubborn, I'll give you that. I think you'll do alright, and woe be to whoever belittles you."

Jito picked up his suitcase from the floor.

"Oh ... and ... one more thing ..." He said, looking around inside the room. "Don't use that phone to make calls. It is really expensive. Fifty cents per minute ... It's an outrage," he added, annoyed, but handed her a fistful of change.

"Go down the street and use the pay phone. It's only twenty-five cents."

"Okay, Jito."

He walked down the stairs and waved his hand back at her. "If things don't go right ... well, you know how to go back to the village."

"Yes, the #12 bus to El Muelle Fiscal and then the Doña Flor to La Palma and then the ..." but he turned, walked down the stairs, and disappeared before she completed the directions back to Chepigana. A minute later he passed the bottom of the stairway pushing the cart full of Seteganti supplies. *I will make it here,* she thought fiercely. *He'll see.*

She got dressed and walked to the payphone down the street, like Jito advised, and laid her one basket of possessions right between her feet. The storm had passed and many people hustled by, girls in skirts and American hairdos she had seen in Ninfa's old magazines, and boys with severe hair all oiled back, watching the girls. All in all, it was a chaotic, busy city, as much this morning as in the middle of the night. She tried to blend in, but people stared at her; she thought she probably stuck out because of her Chocó features. She could almost feel the stares prickling the back of her neck. But their thin-boned almost white faces weren't so pleasing to her either. A few men whistled at her from across the street. She felt heat creep up her neck and rest on her face, hanging there like a dark storm cloud.

"Come on, Elisa, pull yourself together." She fumbled in her worn out pocket for a twenty-five-cent coin and inserted it into the shiny slot to the right of the phone. She dialed the number. "Hello." A bored female voice answered.

"Hello!" she said, relieved for some inexplicable reason. "Can you hear me?"

"Yes, I can," the voice said. Elisa could hardly hear her, the buses were zooming past, people were talking and laughing, and music was drifting in from somewhere, but it was also loud.

"Oh, okay, um, I am Elisa. Jito gave me your phone number."

"Sure, no worries, Elisa. I already know everything. We only have three minutes to talk before your payphone charges you again. So, listen carefully."

She nearly jammed the phone into her right ear. With her free hand she tried to cover her ear against the street sounds. The bus engine noise was unbearable. Who could even think of setting a payphone next to a bus stop?

"Take the bus that says Concepción - Juan Diaz. You will stop in about forty-five minutes at a store called …"

"You need to insert more coins," interrupted the machine.

"No worries," said the lady, calmly but no longer bored. "Do you have five balboa with you?"

"Yes, in fact, I do."

"Take a yellow taxi and give him the address El Nance 39. I will be waiting for you outside. My name is Pruden …"

Elisa heard a long beep. They had gotten disconnected. And then she saw the Concepción bus whiz past. She muttered to herself, "Okay, you're okay, Elisa. Just walk back to the hotel and get a taxi there, okay. You can do it."

She slung her basket over her shoulder and walked back toward the El Sol Hotel, passing by the endless roar of the busy street. Traffic was a blur of multi-colors of cars zooming past her, causing her hair to lift off around her face. In spite of herself, she smiled a little and waited for a slightly slower yellow blur to come by. When one did, she yelled, at the top of her lungs, "Taxi!" It shocked her that it actually stopped.

She stepped into the car, which was filled with smoke from the driver's cigar and made her cough. The driver didn't care. He just blew another big cloud at the windshield. "Where are you going, young lady?"

She looked at the paper again then spoke loudly over the traffic, "Concepción." The music in the car was so loud. The taxi had two big speakers in the back seat, so big that the vibrations coming off of them were shaking the car. I guess city people like loud music, she thought. I suppose I'll learn to like it. But she had a moment of missing the flute and drum of her family's Chocó ceremonies.

Another person on the street was waving his arms frantically to get into the taxi, without noticing that Elisa was already in the back seat. He almost leapt onto the hood but the driver swerved and he flew off into the street. "Idiot," grumbled the driver without a backward glance.

The taxi driver drove away from the center of town to a route by the bay. The windows were open and the wind lapped at her face. She enjoyed the feeling of the sun on her cheek combined with the cool breeze. She could smell the bay, the seawater wafting in and bringing a different kind of air to the city. Couples held hands on the sidewalk, and mothers were busy with three, four, or five kids of all different ages. Elisa was glad to see a different softer side of Panama City.

They turned back away from the water and got to Concepción faster than she had anticipated.

"We're almost there," the driver said. "What is the street name and house number?"

"Oh, um," She checked the small piece of paper again, tucking a wayward strand of hair behind her ear. "El Nance 39."

She looked outside the window again and found that the scene had almost completely changed. No more seagulls, no salty air, no couples holding hands, nor comically overwhelmed mothers. Instead, roads were marked with holes and puddles, there were crowded houses made of wood and cinder blocks, and sometimes even scraps of metal. Scruffy dogs roamed freely. People were sitting outside their houses drinking coffee on makeshift porches. There were kids in uniforms walking to school down those pockmarked streets, some of them barefoot or with holes in their navy-blue skirts and pants. Dust had turned their white shirts beige.

"Hey, slow down!" one boy yelled, slapping the taxi's door.

"Yeah, well you watch where you're going, stupid kid!" the driver yelled right back. "Freakin' Indians," he muttered under his breath, and she felt a pang in her heart.

There were too many holes in the street to avoid them all, so he gunned the engine and hit them all straight on.

"You splashed my white socks, you crazy man! Learn how to drive!" yelled a girl in pigtails on the side of the road; she had plastic bags wrapped around her shoes to protect them from mud. Unfortunately, her socks weren't covered, and they had now turned dirt-brown.

The driver stopped at an intersection, where the main road diverged onto an even narrower and muddier one, which she really hadn't thought possible. The driver stopped and merely sat there.

"I can't go on that street."

"Why not?"

"The condition is horrible. I would get stuck. So, you will have to walk from this point. You will take that street." He pointed with his finger. "About five to seven houses to the left is where you're going."

"How much do I owe you?"

"Nine-fifty."

"That is incredibly expensive, I was told five …"

"Listen, pay me or I beat you, girl. Do it."

Shocked, she scrounged in her purse for the large sum and gave it to him, and then he promptly drove away.

"Elisa!" She heard her name called. There was a lady with wavy black hair down to her hips waving at her from a distance.

"Elisa!"

She waved back tentatively and started to walk towards her when the woman held up her arms and said, "No, stay there!"

She came closer, and Elisa saw that she was wearing shiny black boots that contrasted with the dull brown mud encrusted around the soles. "Are you Prudencia?"

"Yes. Let me get that basket," Jito's sister said, reaching for it.

"Oh, no, that's okay. I can …"

"Listen, child, it rained a lot last night. It was pretty much a hurricane, and I don't want you to get your things dirty. Come to the edges, you can step on the grass instead of the mud."

She walked behind her, quiet, her mind zooming everywhere at once, but as soon as she stepped inside the thatched house, all of it completely stopped as she smelled the abundance of food. "Are you hungry?"

Prudencia read Elisa's mind. "Come to the kitchen."

The kitchen was bright. It had two big glass windows, making the room welcoming.

"Here, grab anything you want to eat. I usually cook once a day and place the food here on the counter. Whoever wants to eat, they come and serve themselves."

There was so much food in colorful bowls at the counter. Chicken, rice, beans, meat stew, hojalda fried bread, corn tortilla with cheese, pasta with meat balls. "How many people live here?"

"Just my three kids: Omar, Marcello, and Antonio with my husband Rudy and me."

"How old are the kids?"

"Omar is twelve. Marcello and Antonio are eight years old," Prudencia smiled. "They are all rascals." She pointed at the end of counter. "Here I have drinks. I made orange juice and rice juice."

Elisa served herself a little bit of everything and sat at the table. "Thank you for having me at your house."

"You are welcome." Prudencia said. "Well, tell me, young woman, what are your plans here in Panama? Are you going to school? Who is going to help you financially? You are only thirteen, right?"

"Fourteen." She filled her fork with a lot of food twice, put it in her mouth, giving her time to answer.

The table got quiet. She sipped her rice drink.

"I have to work. I mean, I will go to school after I establish myself."

"What could you do for work?"

"Anything," she answered, just to make sure she didn't leave any opportunities out.

"Can you cook?"

She wondered what kind of food Prudencia meant. There seemed to be endless choices in the city. "Yes," Elisa said hesitantly.

"I have my little fonda, which is a little *kiosko*, close to the bus stop. I make fried corn tortillas with cheese, hojaldas, picadillos, which is shredded beef, sandwiches, chicken and beef empanadas," she said, "You could help me if you like."

Elisa was stunned. She gulped down her bite. "Yes, I would love to."

"I have gotten very busy lately. Alright, I will teach you how to do it. But I can only pay you $35 balboas a week."

That sounded like a $100 to Elisa. "It is perfect, Prudencia. Thank you."

"When can you start?"

"Tomorrow? I think I need a day to pause. We just arrived from La Palma last night."

Prudencia smiled. "Of course, child."

Elisa opened her eyes slowly. The room was dark. The lights of the living room were on. She could see it through the transparent white curtain hanging at her door. She looked next to her and Prudencia moved the curtains. She adjusted her eyes.

"Are you awake?" Prudencia whispered.

Elisa sat up in her bed, still deeply exhausted from the journey.

This is much too early, she thought.

"Try not to wake up the troublemakers yet. When they are asleep, it's the only time they are peaceful." She walked back out to the kitchen, treading quietly in order not to wake them up.

Elisa glanced to the bed to the left of her shared by Marcelo and Antonio, Marcelo's head at Antonio's feet. "They look so much alike," she said softly, under her breath.

They had the same tone of skin, the same height, and even the same haircut. The one difference she could pinpoint was that one of them was wearing red shorts and the other was wearing blue. She was going to have a hard time telling them apart.

She caught a whiff of freshly brewed coffee in the kitchen, and it was a comforting smell. She got up and joined Prudencia in the kitchen. Rudy and Prudencia were sitting at the table having breakfast.

"Good morning, Elisa," Prudencia said with a smile and a cup of coffee in her hand.

Rudy grunted something unintelligible receiving a pointed glare from Prudencia.

Elisa flashed a quick smile and a good morning and changed her clothes in the small bathroom. She walked back into her bedroom and quietly placed her folded night clothes on her bed. When she walked back into the kitchen, Prudencia had set down a plate for her. "Sit down, Elisa, eat with us."

"I can't eat this early." Elisa didn't know how to say it without sounding rude. "Can I eat it later?"

"No worries. You're fine. There will be plenty of food, but it will not be as quiet to eat as it is now."

"I will eat then."

"Okay let's go to work!"

They walked toward the kiosko. "It's about five-minute walk. It is a pretty safe walk, but I always have Rudy go with me."

"Yes, it's too dark. You never know who's out there," said Rudy.

When they got to the fonda, Elisa felt jumpy. It was dark and the air was crisper than she expected. A street lamp illuminated the dusty street, casting an orange glow on the potholes and puddles. Prudencia rustled around in her pocket until she produced a set of keys; she selected one square bronze key and handed it to Elisa. "Go ahead, this will open the front door under the awning."

She took the key and stuck it in the lock. She jiggled it around until she felt the lock give and swung the door open. A beam shined in from the streetlight. The walls inside were a light, pretty blue, and there was a mural on the wall opposite the door featuring a beer bottle, amber liquid spilling out of the top of the slender necked bottle.

Prudencia kissed Rudy, who had been watching in a bored silence, and she walked over to Elisa. Rudy walked to the street corner and joined a group of ten or so men standing around.

"What are they doing there?" Elisa asked.

"They are waiting for their first bus. They all have to work."

She pointed toward the bottom of the door. "Here grab that corner and I will grab the other corner. When I tell you to push up, you push up." The door was about seven feet long and they each grabbed an end. "Okay, now!"

The zinc door rolled up, clattering all the way to the ceiling. Across the top of the doorway a sign in bold cursive neon letters said PRUDENCIA'S.

"Good job, Elisa." Jito's sister reached into a cupboard on the right side of the door for a long string. She pulled it, and suddenly artificial light illuminated everything. Elisa didn't think she was ever going to get used to that.

She looked around the small space inside the restaurant. There were chairs sitting upside down on top of tables. "Let's start putting the tables and chairs under the awning, so people can sit outside when they eat." Prudencia said slowly, as though she were talking to a small child.

"Alright, sounds good."

"We have four tables twenty chairs and two long benches."

"Do we do this every morning?"

"Yes ... and every afternoon, I put them back again."

"Why not just leave them out? It would save you work."

"In a perfect world, yes." she laughed. "Someone stole everything I had left outside about three years ago, when I just opened the business." Elisa grabbed one side and Prudencia grabbed the other on each table and bench until they moved them all out and surrounded them with benches and chairs.

"Prudencia, that must have been scary to be robbed."

Jito's sister shook her head fiercely. "Those cowards. It was hard to recover. All my investments were gone. Thankfully, the neighborhood has been very supportive. They like my foods so my business is booming again."

Elisa turned her head toward the window when she caught sight of two beams of lights piercing the dark morning, heading for the little restaurant.

"There is the first bus. That's my cue, you see, tells me that it's 4:30."

Elisa saw the dark bus picking up the passengers, including Rudy. It had an old romantic jingle playing loudly on the bus speakers. Music again! Did it never stop!

"Ok. Let's get ready before the next bus passes by at five. That's when everyone wants breakfast."

Prudencia turned on the stove and filled a deep pot with oil. "Here on top of the counter, see the dough to fry the hojaldas. We mix it up the night before." She showed Elisa how to throw flour on the counter, knead it and break off balls to flatten and fry.

A few customers trickled in after they got off the same bus that Rudy got on. She was still kneading the dough, trying to make it less tough. "This is a big ball of dough. It's five times the size of my head." She tore off a piece of the dough and started rolling it around in her palms, making it into rough spherical shapes and setting them down in a row by the others that she had already made. She had about fifteen of the balls of dough to her right, of varying sizes. "How many of these do you make every day?" Elisa asked, her arms already hurting.

"We make about three hundred a day." Prudencia joined her to speed up the production.

Elisa watched as Prudencia quickly and efficiently rolled out the dough and piled them up, and suddenly was ashamed by how slow she was going. "I'm sorry, Prudencia, I can't believe I'm going so slow, I ..."

"Hey, child, it's okay. You'll get much faster as time goes by." She grinned, not unkindly, and suddenly Elisa was filled with warmth.

"How many little balls do you have in that pile?" Prudencia asked, pointing her flour-covered finger at it. She also had a smudge of flour on her forehead fading into her hair.

"Oh, well, let me see, I haven't counted them yet …" Quickly she counted them up under her breath, and said, "I have twenty-three."

"Oh, that will be plenty for the first round of hojaldas." Prudencia put them all in a hand painted bowl and bustled over to a pan of hot oil. "Come here, let me show you how to cook them."

Elisa already knew how to fry bread, of course; she had been making yam-cassava fry-bread since she was seven, but she stayed quiet in order not to overstep her boundaries. "First, you take the ball of dough and you stretch it out until it is long on all sides and flat," that was new to Elisa, "like this, see? Then you drop it in the oil carefully and wait for it to puff up. Then you flip it with these tongs. See?" Prudencia grinned. "Easy."

"Okay, I think I got it."

They spent a little while silently stretching the hojaldas and cooking them then Prudencia spoke up. "You know, time goes by fast here, in this little glorified shack. It's mine, and I love my job, every minute of it. My feet hurt at the end of the day, but when I'm working here, I don't mind it at all. Don't even notice. I just like making people happy and well-fed before they go to work. It's …" She tilted her head to the side, trying to think of the word she wanted to use. Elisa watched her struggle for the word. Elisa knew she found it when her face lit up. "Satisfying. My work is satisfying for me."

Nine hours later, Elisa's feet began to ache, and she said so to Prudencia.

"Oh, you're not used to standing up for this long, I should've made you take a break earlier. Sit down, sit down, I am making food for the two o'clock lunch rush, it's almost ready."

Elisa gratefully sat down at a table that she had just cleaned. Prudencia came and set a bowl of soup down in front of her, the smell making her mouth water. She hungrily wolfed it down. It was hot and tasted like heaven on earth. "This is so good, Prudencia. What is it?"

"That is chicken feet soup. People love it around here. Big profit from it."

"I can see why."

Back at El Nance 39 after a long day at work, Elisa finally had the chance to unpack her basket of belongings. I should have brought more shorts than skirts, she thought, Oh, well. I'll just have to learn how to take the bus to the city to buy some after my first week. She re-folded the first skirt and placed it in a drawer that Prudencia gave her. The dresser had five drawers. Prudencia made Marcelo move all his underwear and clothes to the last three drawers so she could have the top two to herself.

She finished unpacking and tipped the basket upside down. An envelope fell out. Puzzled, she stooped to pick it up. It said, *Read me after two months in Panama City ~ Ninfa*." There was something inside beside a letter. "What's this?" Elisa wiggled the envelope around to get a better feel for it. "Hmmm ... It is something small." She walked over to the lightbulb and held the envelope to the light, trying to make it transparent. To her dismay, it didn't become see-through. "I guess I'll have to wait two months ... Great!" She muttered under her breath. She lifted her small mattress and slipped it underneath, secure that it wouldn't fall out or be touched by mischievous twins. Two months seemed a long time to wait. When she replaced the mattress, she collapsed onto her bed, exhausted. The glass window was open halfway, and a light breeze was lazily moving the curtains. The repetitive movements and the warm air lulled Elisa to sleep. A few minutes more on her feet and she probably would've passed out anyway.

Elisa stood in front of the enormous ball of dough again. Making tiny balls. This time, she brought them herself to the fry pot.

"Look at you girl," said a customer sitting at the table. "Two weeks working with Prudencia and you are faster than Speedy Gonzalez." His four friends sitting with him laughed.

Prudencia smiled and pointed at the sky. "Well ... Do you see what is coming down?" The sun was hiding behind a thick grey cloud.

"Oh no, rain!"

"Rain is fine, girl. It means good business for us. The government hasn't put a roof on the bus stop in years. So, people come under Prudencia's roof to keep dry, and of course they get hungry." Prudencia laughed with delight as the customers helped cluster all the tables and chairs under the awning and inside, close together but still comfortable.

"We had the bus stop roofed but a huge tropical storm came and wiped it out. The roof ended up at the church courtyard," a customer said.

"Kept God dry, anyway," said another.

"How long ago was that?" Elisa asked.

"Seven long years ago," said Prudencia.

Luckily, the bus arrived before the storm, but it looked like few passengers had an umbrella. Then the rain poured down and Prudencia was right. The weather brought more customers than Elisa had ever before seen in the restaurant. People had to stand to eat their hojaldas and quesadillas. Twice as many people squeezed onto the long benches.

"It is ridiculously busy," she grumbled and tossed bread dough into two pots of oil.

"Yes, luckily the twins are off today. I don't like them walking home when it's raining. I swear, they get into every single puddle. Sometimes, I even have to throw their shirts away. No matter how much I wash them, I can't get the brown mud stain out. Plus, they get to help around here." Prudencia grabbed a receipt book and handed it to me.

"Elisa, ask Marcelo to charge that table."

She went inside the little family room behind the kitchen. Marcelo and Antonio were listening to a radio.

"Marcelo." Elisa said to the one with red shorts. "Your mom wants you to charge that table." She pointed at a table under the awning. "Here is the receipt book."

He got up from a little bench. He passed her stretched out arm and flicked the paper in my fingers. "I am not Marcelo." He said while moving a wire hanger on the radio until they heard the voices behind static sounds.

"Marcelo?" she said to the same twin sitting to the same bench. He had on blue shorts and he was wearing the white school shirt. The buttons were undone; the front of his shirt was wide open.

"I am Antonio." The boys guffawed.

The static stopped; a song rang out loud and clear. "There!" The sitting twin yelled at his brother wiggling the antenna. Red-shorts sat down again.

"Here." I dropped the receipt on Red-shorts' lap. "Whoever you are ... go do it!" She walked out.

"Elisa," Prudencia called out as soon as she walked back into the fonda, "take the order of that table, please," she pointed at a table in the corner. "I am behind." She tossed her the little notepad.

"Good morning, what would you like to eat?" She greeted the four men at the table.

"I'd like two hojaldas, one tortilla con queso, and coffee."

"Same."

"Same."

"And you, sir?" Silence.

She turned to see why he hadn't answered. He was staring at her with astonishing blue eyes.

"What would you like?"

"What is your name?"

"I am Elisa. I've never seen you around here."

"I don't live here, but I'm going to be working on an aqueduct. A project for Panama City. These streets are in pretty bad shape and really need drainage."

Elisa shook her head, not knowing how to follow his conversation and distracted by his full lips. She was hypnotized but found her voice. "How long is the project is going to last?"

"About three months. Hopefully more."

"Elisa, hon," Prudencia called.

"Oh, I'm sorry, I'm holding you back." He ran his hand over his brown, curly hair. It was wet.

"Just coffee for me." She turned and walked away about two steps. He added, "Elisa, I am Candelario, by the way."

Glancing back over her shoulder, she smiled at the blue-eyed man.

The day finally ended. "I can't believe they ate twice as much hojalda dough!" Elisa exclaimed. "Do we need to make double for tomorrow?"

"We did good today," said Prudencia. "We did good. I don't think it'll be so bad tomorrow … unless it still pours rain."

Luckily, the twins helped to clean up. Prudencia had ordered them to stop being lazy and unplugged the old radio. After the late lunch hour many hustled home to prepare their houses for the storm and only a few customers came in for dinner. They closed up and went home earlier than usual during a lull in the storm.

"Change your shoes, Elisa," said Prudencia. "It will be muddy."

"Oh, I didn't bring extra shoes."

"I will give you a piggy back ride for seventy-five cents," said Blue-shorts.

"Seventy-five cents is too much!"

"I'll do it for fifty cents," said Red-shorts.

"Deal! Who are you?"

"Marcelo."

"I knew it!"

Elisa got a jolly piggyback ride home. They giggled a lot but half the way to El Nance 39 Marcelo looked tired. He turned to his brother. "Do you want to do the other half? I'll give you twenty-five cents." Antonio swung her onto his back and trotted from there to the house. Even though she was worried they would drop her, Prudencia and the boys got Elisa home with clean shoes.

Elisa slowly felt her body, the pillow under her neck, and humid warmth on her feet. She opened my eyes. A bright ray of morning sun visited the bed.

I haven't seen the sun lying on this bed for a long time. What a luxury. Thank God it's Sunday, she mused and listened to roosters crowing and kids playing outside. She heard a neighbor's steps passing through the alley next to the window and then looked at her roommates' bed. "They're up already," she said softly and remembered. "Oh fun! I get to go the city to buy some clothes." Elisa had saved six weeks of pay: two hundred and ten balboas.

She dressed quickly, in case a twin walked in any minute. "Good morning." She walked in to the kitchen lured by Prudencia's amazing coffee with milk and sugar.

"Good morning," said Rudy. "Have a seat. I am taking care of the kitchen today. I'm giving you all a break."

"Thank you!" Elisa said as she sipped her coffee. She noticed Rudy's skin had become darker since she arrived three weeks ago. He had been working all day every day on an outdoor construction project exposed to the sun. His skin color was chocolate brown and less like *café con leche*. "How is work?"

"Work is good. We finished the demolition of one of

the oldest buildings in Chorrillo." He grabbed two tamales from the red plastic bowl and placed them on a ceramic plate for me. "We start building tomorrow."

Elisa grabbed the knife and cut the strings holding the green banana leaf that wrapped the tamale. She unwrapped the leaf and the aroma of ground corn seasoned with tomatoe sauce filled the room. The tamale held the shape of the unwrapped leaf. Elisa cut it in half, exposing a piece of chicken, a couple of green olives, and a prune. She closed her eyes as she savored the delicious breakfast.

Prudencia walked in. Rudy's face broke into a loving smile. "Here, baby. Sit down. I was telling Elisa all about the new building. I will have at least four months of guaranteed work."

"That's great. We can start saving to build another room in the backyard for Elisa."

"You have been so kind to me, Prudencia." Elisa said. "You haven't even let me pay you for staying here."

"Save your money, hon. You are family from Seteganti. Next year I want you to go back to school."

"But I need to work!"

"You could help me around the house and the kiosko after school. Education is everything for a woman these days."

"Yes, I think so, too." Elisa nodded and filled her mouth with more tamale.

"She is right!" said Rudy.

"So, what are you guys are going to do today?"

"I am taking Elisa to the downtown stores to get new shoes and shorts," said Prudencia.

"Are you excited?"

"Yes, the last time I went shopping, it was for my people in the village six weeks ago. Nothing for me."

"It's going to be fun!" said Prudencia. "You work hard. You deserve to treat yourself, young lady."

Prudencia and Elisa stood at the Concepción bus

stop. There were two others waiting for the bus. Prudencia's blue kiosko looked tidy from the bus stop with its windows and side door closed up tight.

Prudencia looked at her watch. "The bus should be here any minute ...."

"Yes, it's a little late already," a man interrupted.

"I think I heard it." Elisa looked up the hill. "I see it! There, it's turning the corner."

"I am glad. I'm sweating. It is hot and sunny again," said Prudencia holding her flower purse to block the sun from her face. "I almost wish for another storm!"

The red bus came down the little hill. Above the windshield, tt said, "JUAN DIAZ- CONCEPCION."

"You haven't taken the bus yet, have you, Elisa."

"No. Just a taxi."

The bus stopped right in front of them with a squeal of brakes. The door flopped open. "Step right up," the cheerful driver said. The driver extended his hand. "We are two," Prudencia said and gave him fifty cents.

Elisa walked toward the back, looking at the adds over the seats. And the ceiling was covered with beautiful landscapes. "Wow, beautiful art."

She sat down on an empty bench, sliding over to the window. Prudencia sat next to her. "Just relax and enjoy the ride. It is going to take about a half hour." The music was loud, of course. It was an old romantic song.

Elisa looked out the window while the bus moved toward each bus stop, about five minutes apart. She looked at the people getting on and off the bus. She marveled at their different styles —from a person in loose wrinkled clothing to executives looking so trim in suits and ties. Everyone seemed to know each other, or at least be polite.

"Hey, Cassandra." yelled one elderly lady walking toward the back of the bus. "Did you save me a seat?"

"I did. Hurry!" another lady responded.

Elisa watched them hug warmly and then she looked out the window at the city again. The image of a face came to her suddenly. Oh, it was the one with incredible blue eyes. The aqueduct builder at the restaurant. She closed her eyes slowly. He is so handsome, she thought, but she couldn't understand who would name their child Candelario. It was so fancy.

"Stop!" screamed Prudencia disturbing Elisa's reverie. "This is our stop!" The driver slammed on the brakes, everyone jerked forward and back like a dance. Then Prudencia and Elisa easily stepped down to the sidewalk of a busy street full of people.

"There are so many stores." Elisa marveled. There were signs everywhere announcing HALF PRICE or BUY TWO GET ONE FREE or SPECIAL TODAY. Each store had different music blaring from giant speakers. "Who are those beautiful young ladies standing outside the store?"

"They are working girls," said Prudencia with a bit of disdain. "Their job is to get you in and convince you to buy their product."

A woman came over to us. "Come on, hon. We've got a new bathing suit that arrived just today. You'd be the first to show it off on the beach." She held my shoulder tight.

"No, thanks." Elisa said nervously, and Prudencia peeled the woman's fingers from her shirt. Elisa added, "She does smell beautiful, like a mix of flower and coffee." Prudencia had her arm now and kept them walking. I wish I looked like her. I like her style. Tall, curly hair, beautiful smile, Elisa thought. The tan top she's wearing shows off her even brown skin. The d amp air gives her a nice shine.

Prudencia interrupted her thoughts. "You are beautiful, too, Elisa. Don't worry about growing up so fast."

Yet even though Elisa had worked in busy Concepción for six weeks, she was overwhelmed by this part of town with so many stores down each street, music, and clothes.

"Here. Let's go into this store to get your things." Prudencia pointed at a place called Las Bellas. We walked into a maze of displays. People walked around the multiple clothes' stations sometimes grabbing things out of each other's grasp.

"Look at this selection, Elisa. They have lots of kinds of shorts hanging neatly on hangers on a rack. Several lengths, colors, and waistbands. Pick one of each and see which ones you like."

"How much are they?"

"Two balboa each. I think you would like this. The light yellow has a good length about to your knees." She passed it to Elisa.

"Yes, I like it ... and this one too. I like the material." Elisa touched it. "It feels like velvet. I think I like no pockets, a zipper on the side ... fancy." She giggled.

"Not to work, though. Keep the style comfy and simple for cooking... but yes, those would look nice on you. In light blue."

Elisa agreed and picked out green and black shorts along with the yellow and blue. She also found six blouses to match, also two balboa each. She paid the cashier who tried to convince her to buy lipstick, but Prudencia snatched it out of her hand before she could sample some in front of a little mirror.

"How much did you spend?" asked Elisa's new mother-figure.

"All together ... ummm ... twenty balboas." She looked at the big bag she was holding to make sure everything was tucked in carefully. "What else are we doing in this part of town?"

"Let's get some coconut water." There was a cart selling drinks right in the corner of the store.

"How much is the coconut water?" Elisa wanted to seem frugal about her money.

"Twenty-five cents," the vendor said.

She reached for her little wallet but Prudencia pressed it back into her bag. "I'll get it for you, Elisa.

Give me two please."

He filled two paper cups with ice and juice from a big bucket. "Fifty cents, ladies. Have a sip. It's good."

Elisa grinned. "It is so good and fresh."

"Yes, my son just opened the coconuts, young lady." The man chuckled. "My son got busy this morning." He pointed behind him to a young man with a machete opening the coconuts. The young man looked and smiled while pouring the coconut water in the bucket. Next to him was a pile of empty green coconuts. He seemed to enjoy the work.

"Thank you, sir."

They walked down the street with their drinks. Prudencia stopped at the bus stop and yawned. "Well, now let's go back home."

"It was fun." Elisa patted the bag full of her first brand new clothes ever.

Another week passed at Prudencia's kiosko.

"Here is your thirty-five dollars. Finally it's Saturday."

Elisa re-counted her pay for that week. "Twenty ... twenty-five ... and thirty-five." She reached for her special money bag under the sink. She felt it was a safe place since Prudencia covered the pipes under the sink with an oilskin cherry-patterned curtains that wrapped nicely around the cabinet. She took her pouch home at night. "Nobody will take it in fifteen minutes until I finish. I just need to throw the garbage out." She grabbed the garbage bag and walked outside. The sky was grey. The wind and drops of water landed on her legs and back. She rushed inside. "It's pouring outside, Prudencia. And I don't know for how long."

"Well, everything is clean. We might as well sit down and wait until stop raining. I'll make us some warm tea."

They sat down at the table. The rain poured down even harder and the winds picked up speed. Just as they closed the big door and were running back in the front door to get out of the rain, a blue pickup truck pulled up to the curb.

"It's honking," Elisa yelled. "Do you know who it is?"

Prudencia gave the truck a close look. "I think whoever it is wants to give us a ride. But I can't see the driver. I can't even see the PRUDENCIA'S sign. It's raining so hard."

Suddenly, the driver got out with a big black umbrella. He ran toward us. "Come on, ladies. I'll give you a ride." He opened another umbrella for Prudencia ... a smaller one.

Elisa was paralyzed when she saw his stunning blue eyes again. "Candelario," she managed to say. He grabbed her shoulder and smiled. "Come on, Elisa. Get in the truck while I help Prudencia lock up." His voice was sweet and comforting.

She sat between Prudencia and Candelario while he drove through the downpour. "It's going to be a huge storm." He adjusted the mirror and his shoulder pressed into hers.

"Make a right here," said Prudencia. "You have to drop us here or you'll get stuck in the mud."

The street was covered with brown mucky water. Candelario laughed. "I'll take the risk. If I get stuck, we'll walk."

Elisa's feet were soaked from the rain, her new white shoes already turned brown. The truck wheels were spinning.

"Elisa, where do you live so I can take you there."

"I live with Prudencia."

"Oh, I see. Where is your family?"

"They live in Darién. A village called Seteganti. I came to the city to work and study."

"You are a brave young lady."

"This is our house." Prudencia pointed. "The yellow brick one."

Candelario grabbed the umbrella from under the passenger seat. "Let me walk you in first," he said to Prudencia. "Then I'll come back for you, Elisa."

He ran around the front of his car, sloshing through water, opened the door for Prudencia and then walked her to the house, and came back to the truck. "Come on, Elisa." He waited for her to slide out. It was very windy. The umbrella he was holding flipped backward. The strong heavy rain got into the cab and Elisa slipped. He held her very close so she wouldn't blow away, too. She smelled his sweet metallic smell as soon as he got close. She had never smelled anything like it before. "Thank you," she said hoarsely and thought, I have never been close to a strange man before. She tried to be graceful he walked slowly toward the house. She didn't want to rush even through the storm. She wanted to feel his strong warm body. She wanted to smell his breath.

He released her on the porch. "Ok, beautiful. Just go inside, please." Candelario said with a grin.

"You can stay, Candelario," yelled Prudencia from inside the house.

Please say yes, Elisa wished as she went into the warm dry house.

Prudencia continued, "It's windy and raining very hard. It is too dangerous for you to get back in your truck."

Rudy went to the door. "It is a full strong tropical storm," said Rudy. "I heard it on the radio. Stay."

Candelario shook out the umbrella and nodded. "Okay. I'll stay. I just don't want to cause any extra work for you all."

"Come in. Come in. Please take this towel and dry yourself." Prudencia extended her arm and handed him a clean towel.

He took the towel and smiled gratefully before putting it on his shoulder. He closed the umbrella and leaned it against the wall.

"I'll make hot chocolate," said Prudencia. "It's going

to be a long night."

The rain poured down for four hours straight. I sat in front of Candelario. Prudencia handed me a blanket with one hand, and she held three long white candles in her other.

"That candle is ready to go out." Pointing at the candle on the coffee table between Candelario and me. "Let me know when it has burned down so I can bring a new one."

She walked away to light more candles around the house.

"I don't think you all are going to work tomorrow," Candelario said. The candle light was shimmering on his face, making a shadow of his silhouette on the wall behind him.

"Probably not," Elisa said.

"So tell me, Elisa ... I know you said you're going to school after this school year ends. What school do you want to go to?"

"I was thinking of learning how to sew. I have seen my cousin's work. She makes good money creating clothes."

"I think it's a great idea," said Rudy while looking for a chair to sit with us. "Elisa, you learn very quickly. You are smart and ambitious. You could make good money."

"My sister is a seamstress. She has a lot of clients, and she complains about being behind in deliveries," said Candelario. "I bet she can use some help."

"Will you ask her?"

"Of course, I will. I'll ask her as soon as I see her." His face faded in the dark.

"Prudencia." called Rudy. "We need another candle. This one went out."

Elisa felt like she had the best luck with people offering her work as soon as she felt ready for it. She was so glad she didn't have to be like the women in front of the clothing stores trying to get people inside by being insistent and bothersome. Her second feeling was hesitation. Prudencia needed her at the busy kiosko. She wanted to be loyal to Jito's sister, who gave her a job her first day in Panama City.

When Elisa woke up in the morning, it was overcast but not raining anymore. Then she remembered Candelario. Was I dreaming? she wondered and thought everything seemed unreal. A noise from the living room sounded upset. Is that Prudencia crying? The storm ... Candelario ... What happened? Scared, she rushed out of the bedroom.

"Where is Candelario?" she asked immediately.

"He left in the middle of the night," said Rudy. "After you went to bed."

I looked outside. "But his truck is still here."

"He left it here ... He wanted to know if his family was okay. He'll come back for his truck when the roads open up."

I looked at the corner where Prudencia was sitting. "Why is Prudencia crying?"

"I went to the kiosko. Everything is wrecked. The storm flooded it."

"Has Prudencia seen it?"

Rudy sighed. "No... no yet."

"Oh, such bad, bad news." Elisa's heart sunk seeing Prudencia sitting in chair looking out the window, weeping, holding a small towel to her eyes. She sat next to this special woman who worked so hard and was so generous. She rubbed her back and didn't say a word.

Prudencia, Rudy, the twins, and Elisa cleaned up the kiosko. The wood floor was soaked.

"It has been five days already; you would think that with this heat, the water would have evaporated already," grumbled Rudy. He walked through water puddles wearing his black plastic heavy-duty boots. The twins picked up all the zinc roof sheets spread through the yard and street. They piled them up in a corner to be reused to repair the roof.

"Be careful!" said Prudencia. "Marcelo, you are not wearing your gloves. You're going to get cut." Marcelo rolled his eyes at his mother. "Elisa, we need to talk." She walked her toward the couple of chairs they had brought from home, since all the chairs and tables had broken into pieces, as if thrown across the restaurant by an enraged giant. She pulled out a chair. "Elisa, sit please." She wrung her hands and sighed. "I just don't know how to tell you." Elisa looked down at her own hands. The first thing that came to mind was that she would be kicked out of the house. Prudencia continued in a soft voice. "I don't have any money to give you for this week. Tomorrow is your pay day and I don't have that money for you … even though you have more than earned it."

"It's okay, Prudencia. You don't have to pay me. You and your family have been so kind to me. And my savings survived." Elisa showed her the waterlogged pouch that she had looked for in a panic under the sink when they first arrived at the ruined PRUDENCIA'S. It had been jammed behind the sink so tightly it didn't budge.

"It has been wonderful working with you and teaching you, Elisa. You learned so quickly. I mean ... I'm glad you have some savings, but you're always welcome to stay with us. You'll just have to find another job."

Elisa felt such relief. She stood and hugged her friend and second mother ... or third after Ninfa. "I'll stay with you, Prudencia. Thank you. And I can still help in the house while I find another job. I have enough savings that I can share with you for now. Do you want me to help buy food?" She held the wrinkled damp leather across her hands like an offering.

"I am touched by your generosity, but no worries, child. I have savings, too." Prudencia laughed with her first delight since the storm, delight that they were all going to be okay. "Plus, Rudy is working. God will provide."

Elisa held her hand. "We will get through this together, Prudencia. You aren't alone."

"I'm hungry!" yelled Antonio from the kitchen.

"Let's go home for dinner. Then, we can come back to clean more up before it gets dark." Prudencia and Elisa walked out together with arms linked.

Chapter Five
Needle and Thread

Elisa sat with Prudencia out on the porch. It was an intense summer evening. One week they had a raging storm, the next one an excruciating wave of heat. It had been five weeks since the tropical gale but the whole town still talked about it as if it had happened yesterday.

Elisa was sweating like the lemonade pitcher sitting on the table. She saw a person near the blue truck parked in the front yard. Candelario came to mind, the night he stayed with them. She had never stopped thinking about him. "Is that Candelario?"

Prudencia nodded. "I guess he's finally come to get his truck."

Elisa was hoping for more than that, hoping that he was coming to see her too. She and Prudencia stood as he came up on the porch and hugged them both.

He sat as Prudencia went to get him a glass for lemonade. "So nice to see you, Elisa. I have good news for you."

"What?"

"My sister needs your help. She has lots of new customers since the storm ... I guess a lot of people had their clothes ruined and waterlogged. After I told her how hard you've worked for Prudencia, she offered to pay you fifty balboa a week to help her with her work."

Elisa clapped her hands and would have jumped up and down but she didn't want to seem childish. Instead, as Prudencia came back out, she calmly said, "Good news, Prudencia, I'm going to start a new job."

Prudencia tipped her glass towards me with a smile.

"Wait." Elisa looked at Candelario directly. "Does she know that I don't have experience? I don't want to be more trouble than I'm worth."

"She knows ... and she'll call Prudencia for a reference but I told her everything I know about your journey here, which is pretty remarkable." He held her face between his two hands. Elisa was stunned and delighted. "When do you want to start?"

She could hardly speak while he was touching her but she managed to mutter, "Tomorrow?"

"Okay. I'll pick you up tomorrow early in the morning to introduce you to each other." The phone rang in the house. "That's probably her calling now."

Prudencia stood up with a grin and went in to answer the call.

Next morning, Candelario picked her up in the blue truck. It was still dark. Prudencia handed them two cups of *café con leche* in paper cups.

He broke the silence. "Are you nervous?"

"Just a little."

"There is nothing to worry about. Marty is as sweet as honey ... just like you." He looked at her and smiled. She felt her face warm up and her hands sweat.

"How do I get to your sister's on my own? I know you're not going to be able to give me a ride every day."

"I'll be happy to give you a ride every time I can ... but you're right, I work every day all day. For all its problems, Panama City has a good bus system," he added. "I wish you were older ... so you could drive yourself to work."

"Oh, I see." She sipped her coffee but was bothered by his answer. She didn't want him to see her as a youngster.

"It's easy to get there. You take one bus for about forty-five minutes, get off here, walk up this small hill." He turned to the right, drove up a hill with little houses on either side of a brick road, and found a parking spot. "Here we are. I'll introduce you to my sister."

He went around his truck and opened the door for Elisa. They walked down the block in the dawn light. The rising sun already felt warm, foretelling another hot day. It wasn't too humid but Elisa's hair was tangled from the wind through the truck. As she tried to comb it with her fingers she tripped on a loose brick.

"Watch out," said Candelario catching her arm and shaking his head. "This street can injure your ankle. They need some serious repairs." He held her arm close to his body and they walked over to a sidewalk. "There it is." He pointed at a white house. They walked to a green door and Candelario knocked vigorously. Elisa heard the sound of flip flops approaching from inside.

A voice grumbled. "I'm coming. Who in the world is knocking this early? Somebody better be dying." A hard sound of a metal latch snapped. A woman opened the door, but only half; the lower part remained closed. Elisa could only see her from waist up with a decorative wall behind her filled with little colored lights. She could also see a Virgin Mary on an altar with lit white candles attached to the wall.

"Ah, it's you. I forgot you were coming." She went from grumpy to laughter in an instant. She reached to the wall and turned on a light. Elisa could see her welcoming smile from the lamp illuminating her face. She didn't look like Candelario and she was even shorter than Elisa. "I'm sorry," she brushed her short wavy black hair with fingers just like Elisa had done a few minutes earlier. It made Elisa like her right away. "Excuse my night gown."

"Oh, no worries ... you're in your home. I'm Elisa."

"I'm Martina, or Marty. Come on in, please." Marty opened the lower half of the green door.

"Well, I got to get going, ladies. I have to go work now."

"You just got here." Candelario stayed outside of the door. "But I understand, brother. How are your two boys doing?" Marty asked.

I was surprised by that question. I gulped and asked, "Boys?"

This time he stepped inside the house.

"They are doing good ... growing."

"They must be crawling by now," said Martina.

"They're all over the place." Candelario looked at me

without saying a word. He looked at his watch on his wrist.

"I do need to go. Elisa, you're in good hands. I'll come and check on you soon." He hugged me. I smiled a little uncertainly.

"It's only seven. Normally I start working at eight," said Marty. "Make yourself comfortable. There's some coffee in the kitchen. The radio news starts in forty-five minutes." She walked toward a room just as Candelario left the house.

Elisa sat on a chair in Martina's workshop looking at different customer accounts. This was her first assignment. The blue portfolio was filled with lined papers. She was looking for a customer that Marty asked her to find.

"Oscar Nuñez," she read on the label.

"Yes, that's him," Marty sat at her old sewing machine stitching together two pieces of pink fabric.

"He's been with you since ... 1928. Twenty years."

"Yep." Marty laughed. "He is a regular for sure ... and my ex-husband. I lost the husband but kept the client. At least, we got one thing right." I heard someone knock at the door in the front of the house. "Oh, speak of the devil."

"I'll open the door." Elisa offered. She walked out of the sewing room and crossed the dark living room lit only by a string of little lights to get to the split-in-half door. Oddly, the room had no windows. Natural light came in the living room only from the door. So opposite from the tambo that had no walls and was all light, at least in the day. Elisa chuckled.

"Who is it?" She asked before opening the latch.

"Oscar."

She unlocked the lower and upper parts of the peculiar door and opened the top half. He looked surprised to see a strange face. "And who are you?"

"I am Elisa, Marty's new helper." I felt a bit shy. "Today is my first day on the job."

"It's about time she got some help. Open the rest of the door, please." As he walked back to the shop, he said, "Now, she has no excuse not to finish my pants on time."

"There you are," said Marty. "Elisa, hand me the tape measure," she pointed at the table full of different fabrics and scissors. She grabbed a pink tape for her new boss. Marty got up and showed me her notes under Oscar's account.

"His measurements change every year." He grumbled behind them. "I don't want to take a chance. Write here his waist size and here his height from foot to waist," she instructed. "When we're done with Oscar, I'll show you the fabric shelves and then we'll finish for today. I'll let you go early."

"That sounds good. That way I can find my way back to Concepción."

Prudencia, Rudy, and Elisa had a nice dinner while Antonio and Marcelo sat on the sofa doing homework and listening to the radio. Elisa felt so comfortable with this family but right now her thoughts drifted to Candelario. She thought of him a lot, especially his kindness, the way he cared for her. She hoped she'd see him again soon ... even knowing he had children.

"Elisa, you haven't touch your food." Prudencia brought her back from her thoughts. "Did you learn a lot today from Marty?"

"Yes, Marty showed me how to keep her customer accounts, how to take measurements, and how to keep the fabric organized in her storage. She said that I'll be doing this all week to get familiar with the basics. Plus, she needs help with that the most."

"Do you like it?"

"I like it so far ... Can I ask you a question?"

"Sure."

"Did you know that Candelario has two babies? What do you know about him?"

"I know about as much as you do about Candelario,

Elisa." Prudencia frowned. "All I know is that he works for the crew of government engineers to repair streets. That's about it," She looked at Elisa for a few seconds. "Two kids are not a problem. The problem will be if there is a wife."

It never crossed my mind that he would be with somebody. I felt a rush of disappointment.

"Elisa, how old is he? In his twenties, don't you think?" Prudencia asked.

"I don't know."

"Elisa, you are thirteen, aren't you?"

"Fourteen. I'll be fifteen soon, I think." Elisa looked away. "But we don't really keep birth records in the village, so it could be off by as much as a year. I could be older."

"No matter. You shouldn't worry about an older man. Focus on what you're here for. You left Seteganti to have a bigger life. Remember how you felt about Jito and the girl in La Palma? Don't take your eyes from the prize. *Your* prize. You're smart."

"Oh, don't worry. I'm going to go to school and work and ..."

"Good, I'm glad." Prudencia turned to the boys. "Have you two finished your homework?" They nodded "Come and eat. It's eight thirty already."

Elisa had some questions to ask Candelario. What am I thinking? she reflected. He is probably happily married and just a good guy who felt pity for me.

"I am going to shower, Prudencia." She got up from the dining table. "Then, I'll help you clean up and go to bed. I have to catch an early bus tomorrow."

All day long Marty and Elisa were busy measuring fort fifteen young ladies' *quinceañeras* party dresses plus the quinceañera birthday girl's frock. Elisa had to have two tape measures; one in her hand and the other around her neck just in case she lost the one she was holding.

"Well, young ladies. We're all set. Come back in two weeks so we can follow up with a fitting." The girls were about fourteen years old. All getting their clothes on, giggling. It was so hard to find anything because they had just thrown them around the fitting area.

"Marty, where did I put the portfolio? I need to write the measurement for the last girl."

"I don't know, hon. Write it on a piece of paper. We'll find it later. You won't be able to find it now in this mess."

The girls left, and finally, there was peace and quiet in the house. Then there was a knock on the door. "Another customer?" Elisa slumped. "I hope not. I am exhausted. I've worked six hours straight for someone else's birthday on my own birthday."

"No, it's not a customer." Marty looked at her young worker. "It is a late lunch delivery to us."

"Oh, really? Thanks. I was in the hurry this morning and I forgot my lunch."

She started toward the front door but Marty stopped her. "I got it, Elisa. My treat. It's your birthday, after all. Prudencia called me and told me."

"Oh, okay I'll set the table then." Elisa grabbed two plates, forks, knives, and two cups. She brought them to the table in one trip and set it up quickly while Martina paid the delivery guy.

"Thank you, ma'am. Enjoy," said the delivery girl after seeing the nice tip Marty had dropped in her hand. Marty placed the food on the table. She'd bought fried rice, chicken soup, some aromatic shrimp, vegetables, and white rice. "Let me serve you some of this fried rice. It is so good."

"Where is this restaurant?"

"It's right on the corner. A Chinese couple own it. They've been in business for twelve years."

I tried the fried rice. "Wow. It's so good. The chicken, the shrimp, the ham, the vegetables— everything smells so amazing."

"I told you! Happy Birthday, Elisa."

"Thank you. I remember back at the village my parents—before they disappeared—my Aunt Ninfa, too, always celebrated for me." She smiled softly. "They made sweets. Every year ... I swear, they used the same candles." Now, her thoughts were drifting toward Candelario; she wished he was here, but he was probably with his family. He hadn't been around for a week.

"Thank you for lunch. I do appreciate you, Marty."

"You are welcome." She pointed at my plate with her fork. "Enjoy it."

Elisa took the bus home after this busy day of work then walked down El Nance. Close to the house, she saw a blue pickup truck outside. Her heart skipped a beat. Candelario! She whispered, "This could be my best birthday present. I'm so happy." She walked faster toward Prudencia's house thinking, Oh, I am going to see him.

Outside, Candelario walked toward his truck. He opened the door with his keys. He pulled out a present wrapped with beautiful white and pink wrapping. Elisa had reached the front yard. "Hi."

He turned around with a grin. "This is for you." He handed her the present. "Happy Birthday." He hugged her.

"How did you know today was my birthday?"

"Marty told me." He grabbed her shoulder with his big hand. "Come on. Everyone is waiting for you inside."

"Who is waiting for me ... Why?" But when Elisa stepped into the living room. Everyone yelled in unison. "Happy Birthday!"

The twins, Prudencia, Rudy, and a couple of neighbors stood around the table. There was a white round cake with pink roses and little yellow candles.

After they finished the birthday song *Las Mañanitas*, Prudencia pulled her to the table. "Make a wish and blow out your candles."

Okay. Make a wish, Elisa, she said to herself,

leaning close to the cake. She looked at all the loving faces and exclaimed, "Oh, I have so many ... which one do I want most!" She felt Candelario next to her. I want Candelario to love me and be with me forever, Elisa wished and blew all the candles out.

"Thank you all. This is ... wonderful and sweet!" She was too emotional to say anything else.

"You are fourteen—or maybe fifteen—now, Elisa," said Prudencia. "Let me give you the first piece of cake," She cut it and put it on the plate for her.

Elisa savored the first bite. "It is so creamy ... mmm. I can taste the milk, and the fresh strawberries are delicious. Thank you, Prudencia."

"Thank Candelario. He was the one who brought it."

"I want a piece," said Marcelo grabbing a plate and lifting it for Prudencia to cut some for him.

She swatted him back. "Wait! Let me cut all the pieces for everyone."

Candelario nudged her. "So, do you want to open the present now?"

"Yes, I do." Elisa picked up the box, shook it, but didn't hear anything. "What is it?" she asked in wonder.

"Why don't you open it?"

"Ok. I'll be right back. There's not enough space to sit down."

She walked into the bedroom and placed the present on her bed then carefully stroked the beautiful pink ribbon around the box.

Candelario walked in. "Can I come in?"

Elisa didn't respond for a while. "It's not even my bedroom."

"Well, you deserve a bedroom of your own."

"I've never had a room just for me." Elisa looked straight into his blue eyes. "Why are you so nice to me, Candelario?"

He looked away and said. "Are you going to open the present or not?"

"Oh, yes, of course." She undid the wrapping paper

slowly and found the white box inside was taped. Elisa loosened the tape and lifted the top off. Inside white paper wrapped nicely around a lovely white blouse.

"Oh, Candelario. Thank you." Elisa held it to her chest. "I can wear it tomorrow with my new pair of jeans."

"Thank you." He grabbed her face and put it close to his and kissed her close to her lips. "Happy Birthday, Elisa." Antonio trotted into the bedroom to eat his cake on his bed. Candelario stepped back and Elisa felt wonderfully happy.

"This is the best birthday ever."

Six months passed. Elisa had helped Prudencia get her kiosko back together on weekends In spite of the wreckage of the storm, now PRUDENCIA'S didn't look like it had ever been hit.

"Thank you for all you did, Elisa. You are an angel." Prudencia hugged her.

"Anything for you. I'm happy that you got everything back running like it used to be." She paused. "Can I talk to you?"

They sat under PRUDENCIA'S awning. Elisa began, "It's been six months since I started working with Martina. I really like the sewing work, but the problem is getting up so early to catch the bus, and sometimes it is so full. People have to stand because there aren't enough seats."

Prudencia nodded. "I know what you mean."

"So I was thinking maybe I should try to move closer to Marty. There is a lady that has a room to rent just across from Marty. She is renting it for fifty balboas a month, which my salary and my overtime can cover easily."

"I think this is a great idea, hon. You do what's best for you." Prudencia had tears in her eyes. "I will miss you, though. You're part of this family. You're the daughter I never had."

Elisa leaned over and hugged her. "I'll come to visit you, Prudencia. On Sundays. I promise."

A few days later, after finishing work, Elisa and Marty walked down the street to the neighbor's house to look at her room.

"It'll take us five minutes to walk there. She doesn't have kids either. That's also a plus when you're renting. Not so much noise."

"Does she know we're coming?"

"She knows, and she got the room ready for you."

"How old is she?"

"She's in her late twenties. She's a cook and works for a very wealthy family. Her husband is in the construction business. He's a very strong black man."

The cook's building was at the end of the brick street. Elisa took in the details: The apartment was on the first floor. She had a palm tree in a red pot. A pair of boots were drying outside.

Marty knocked at the door. A lovely woman opened it. "Hello! Come on in."

She had the sweetest and tender eyes Elisa had ever seen. She looked at the radiant woman. Her light cocoa skin was in beautiful contrast with her dark hair. Her face was perfect without make up and she had her hair in a bun. "How are you, Marty?"

"I'm alright. Business is going well. It's just too busy to handle it on my own." Marty laughed. "I'm glad to have my new helper."

"I'm Juana," she said. "You must be Elisa."

"Yes." They shook hands. Elisa looked around the nice home. The floor had black and white tiles. The tall window from floor to ceiling gave the place a lot of natural light. "It's lovely in here."

"Oh, thank you. Having a husband that works in construction can come in very handy ... Roberto, honey," she called down a hallway.

"Come here. Come meet Elisa." Roberto came out of the back room. He had shiny black skin. A white shirt was snug around his defined, muscular body. "Nice meeting you, Elisa. How is Marty treating you?"

"Very, very well. I couldn't ask for a better boss."

Marty waved her hand at the compliment. "Well, we're here just for a little bit. Elisa has to take the bus home to Concepción. If she misses it, she'll have to wait for another two hours, and that's why staying here would be so nice for her."

"Alright, so let me show you the room. I hope you like it," said Juana.

Roberto grabbed his jacket off a hook by the door. "I have to go. Hope to see you again, Elisa."

"Ok, hon. I'll see you later." Juana waved as he walked out the door.

The three walked down the hall. All the flooring in the apartment was the same black and white tile. Juana opened a door at the end of the hall. "Here it is."

Elisa stepped into the room and was bombarded with pink. The walls were pink, the small bed was covered with a pink comforter that matched the chair, the night stand lamp and the curtains were pink. "It is *very* pink."

"Robert's mom passed away about a year ago. She lived with us all through her last years." Juana laughed. "She loved pink as you can see. But we could change it for you, Elisa. We can paint it another color."

"No, no. It's perfect. I like it." Elisa was beyond thrilled. "When can I move in?"

"Whenever you want. It's ready for you."

"Can I move in this weekend?"

"Sure, you just have to give me the deposit and first month's rent. I'll make an extra copy of a key for you." She handed Elisa a copy of the lease that lay on the bureau.

Elisa scanned it quickly. "Marty, can you help me understand this?" Marty nodded. "Juana, I have savings. I can sign this and bring you the money tomorrow."

"I know it will all work out well." Juana gave Elisa the most beautiful welcoming smile.

While packing her clothes, Elisa realized her wardrobe had tripled since the day she arrived at Prudencia's with a small basket slung over her shoulder. That basket had held all her worldly possessions. She turned to Prudencia. "I'm shocked. I don't have a big enough case to carry my things. I came here with little more than one skirt and a pair of black boots."

Prudencia chuckled. "Now you're a city woman with a great job, your own clothes, your own money … just what you dreamed in faraway Setegantí. Well, how many suitcases do you think you will need?"

"Probably two small ones or one big one."

"Let me see what I have." She stood in the doorway and hollered, "Marcelo! Go get a taxi for Elisa."

"Oh, no need. Candelario offered me a ride today. He'll be here soon."

"Let me stop Marcelo before he leaves." She ran outside. "Marcelo, never mind!" It was too late; Marcelo and Antonio were racing down the street.

"Am I forgetting anything?" Elisa asked herself. She looked around the room, and glancing at the worn Chocó basket, she remembered what she had found in the bottom of it when she unpacked it in Panama City. "The letter!" She lifted the mattress, amazed it was still there and that she hadn't thought about it for months. She pulled it out and looked at Ninfa's tidy handwriting.

"Elisa, Candelario is here." Prudencia brought her a large leather suitcase. "This should fit everything."

A minute later, Candelario came into the bedroom, looking at his watch. "Let's get going. I have a meeting in an hour."

"I'll be done in a few minutes."

"I'll wait for you outside." Elisa put her personal things and the letter in the Chocó basket and laid her folded clothes in the case. It filled up quickly. "Oh well," she sighed, "I think I have most of it."

Prudencia held her arms across her chest. "No worries, I'll keep anything you forget and give it to you the next time I see you. Hopefully, soon."

She sounded so sad that Elisa stopped packing, pulled open Prudencia's arms, and hugged her one more time. "Thank you, Prudencia. You are an incredible friend."

"Okay, you're going to make me cry now." Prudencia put her hand on Elisa's arm. "Just be careful with Candelario, He's a good man but he's, well, still a man."

"Ninfa warned me about men when I left Setegantí, too."

"Good. So now you're hearing it twice. I see he's getting very close to you and I wonder why. You should too because you still don't know anything about him except that he has two kids and a job."

"We're just friends."

"I know, I know ... just be careful. Mostly of your own feelings."

Elisa snapped the bag shut and swung it off the bed. "Time to go."

Candelario came to the doorway. "Ready yet?" Elisa nodded. "Okay. Let's hustle." Candelario picked up the case and headed to the truck.

Prudencia walked outside with them. "Well, don't be a stranger now."

"No, I won't."

Marcelo and Antonio came back from the main road. "We couldn't find a taxi yet."

"Candelario is going to take her." Prudencia pinched Marcelo's cheek lovingly. "I yelled but you were already flying down El Nance. Now hug Elisa goodbye."

"Bye, Elisa." The twins gave her playful little bear hugs, and she felt so loved.

As Candelario drove them away, Elisa looked back. Prudencia and the twins were still waving good bye. She thought of bumping away with Bo and Jito through the Darien jungle to the Rio Turia. She'd had this basket on her lap then, too, and was a lot more afraid than she let on. But today she wasn't afraid at all.

"Come on in," said Juana. Elisa walked into the house with black and white tiles, Candelario behind her with the big suitcase. "Oh, you brought a helper."

"This is Candelario. Marty's brother."

"Nice meeting you." He shook her hand. "Well, her room is at the end of the hall. Elisa can guide you."

She led him to the room and he stood in the doorway grinning wickedly. "I guess this is completely a girl's room. Where do you want this suitcase? On the pink chair or the pink table or the pink bedspread or in the pink closet?"

"On the floor, which is not pink, in case you noticed."

Juana laughed at them. "I made dinner to welcome you, Elisa. Would you like to stay Candelario?"

"Oh, no. I can't. Thank you, though."

Elisa noticed that Juana projected so much maturity, even though she was almost as young as Candelario.

"Well, I'm off. I'll come to visit soon, Elisa." Then he left in the hurry.

"Nice young man." Juana gazed after him with curiosity. "Are you hungry, Elisa?"

"Yes, I am. I haven't been able to eat anything today. I was a little nervous about the move."

"Change is good, dear girl, and inevitable at your age. Unpack. I'll get the table ready."

Elisa went to her room and sat on the bed. She looked around feeling proud, proud of her courage. The feeling of moving forward was satisfying. Despite uncertainties, she seemed to know how to make good decisions ... receiving plenty of help from good people. "Ninfa's letter!" She opened the basket, grabbed the letter, and opened it. It wasn't long.

"My dear cousin, you by now are probably enjoying the nice beach with a beautiful bathing suit. I don't want to keep you away from the fun. I just wanted to tell you I love you and that we are here for you if you get tired of a fancy life. Here is a little present for you. May God keep you safe. Aunt Ninfa"

Elisa wiped her tears and opened a little tiny envelop that was inside the letter.

"Oh! A golden necklace with a cross pendent." Ninfa had liked going to the little chapel on the edge of Seteganti more than Elisa did. But after the frightening night in the El Sol Hotel when she asked for a voice, Elisa realized there was more to it than just a boring old mass. She had gone to a few services with Prudencia on Sundays, too. The priest talked about some interesting things, like how to handle difficult times. Elisa put on the chain and grabbed the cross with her hands. "Thank you, dear Ninfa." she said, hoping her aunt could feel her gratitude.

Juana knocked at the door. "Dinner is ready."

Juana served the food in a gracious way, no hurry, no wild twins snatching food faster than a monkey. "I hope you like plantains." She passed a crystal bowl full of fruit.

"Oh, I do. Any plantains really. From fried green plantains to the ripe ones. You name it. They're my favorites. We harvested them from the jungle in Darién. When I came to Panama City, we were bringing bags of plantains to sell at the market, along with cassava, maize, cacao, and baskets." Elisa served herself a spoon of white rice and bathed them in black beans.

"Oh, really? That must have been an adventure coming down the river. Did you go to La Palma?"

"Just for a little while. Then we caught a boat from there to the El Muelle Fiscal."

Juana paused and looked at her with concern. "That can be a dangerous place."

"Well, I was there with another trader named Jito. He

knew what to do because he'd been here many times. I was handling the list of supplies for our village."

Juana stared at her. "But you stayed in Panama City?"

Elisa shrugged, now feeling shy. "Well, I wanted to try something different. I've been living with Jito's half-sister. Working in her little kiosko making hojaldas and other food."

Juana tapped the crystal bowl with her fork. "Well, if you like something different, you would love my favorite temptation plantains."

"Temptation plantains?"

"Yes, basically you peel the ripe plantains and cut them in three parts. You fry them with butter, and once the plantains get a golden color, top them with brown sugar, cinnamon, and cranberry juice. They're called 'temptation' because you can't eat just one."

"That sounds delicious. My mouth is watering."

"I'll make it for you soon!"

They ate quietly for a few moments. "Were you born here in the city?" Elisa asked.

"No, I was born in Colón and came to the city when my mom died."

"I am sorry. My … my parents died, too."

"Well, we have that in common. I had three sisters and two brothers. I was the oldest one. I was seven years old when we were placed in foster homes. My caregivers were not as nice as my siblings' foster parents. They made me work until late. Carrying heavy buckets of water," she touched her back over her shoulder. "That is how I got this little hunch in my back."

"Oh, I hadn't noticed. That was really mean." Elisa felt upset that this kind woman had been treated badly.

"It's alright. As soon as I turned sixteen, I left to work on my own. I eventually met Roberto and my life has been much better since then. We've been married for five years now."

"I am glad, Juana. Are you guys planning to have

babies?”

She paused and looked down at the table for a moment. She looked back up. “We’re trying. We both went to the doctor. They couldn't find anything wrong with him. The problem apparently is me … but we’re still trying.” Her voice broke but she let out a long breath. “Do you want something to drink?”

“I’ll get us something to drink, Juana. No worries.” Elisa insisted before she got up. “Now, you have someone to help you around here.”

The fifteen young ladies from the quinceañeras event were excited that the dresses were ready. The dresses hung from the living room ceiling. Some girls were wearing their outfits admiring themselves in the tall mirror on the wall.

“Yours looks better, Evelina,” said a girl named Lucia with a downward twist to her mouth.

“You look very sweet, dear. The dresses are all the same,” said Marty. “What varies is the color. The Sarita’s mom picked light yellow and baby blue. Go tell the mom if you’d rather have blue. But I think yellow brings out the pink in your pretty cheeks.” That made Lucia look at herself again with a smile.

“Alright, girls. I have to be at church for afternoon mass. Grab your dresses. You are all set.” Marty went back to the sewing room to put away tape measures and little pincushions.

Elisa helped a couple of them get their dress off. The gaggle of girls skipped out to two big cars outside waiting for them.

I closed the double doors. “Finally, silence.”

“I have to go, Elisa.” Marty came out of her bedroom holding a purse. “Close the door when you leave. Don't worry about the mess. I’ll clean it up when I come back.”

“I’ll clean it up. No worries.”

“See you tomorrow, hon.”

Elisa stayed alone, puttering and putting things away.

She put soft music on the radio. She didn't mind the work at all. She lived so close there was no hurry to catch a crowded noisy rush-hour bus.

Then someone broke her peace by knocking loudly on the front door. Elisa hoped a girl hadn't returned for something. She wasn't in the mood for more chatter. She hesitantly opened the top half door. "Candelario! Hi!"

"Can I come in?"

"Sure. Your sister isn't here, though."

"She won't mind." He smiled. "I brought you *tres leches*. You're working hard. I want to take you for dinner but I know that you eat with Juana every night. So ... here." He handled me the bag. "You can share this dessert with Juana and Robert."

"Thank you. They'll be delighted." They stood in the middle of the now tidy living room but she noticed he looked a little weary "What's wrong?" she asked him. "Are you working too hard?"

He sat down with a thump in an armchair. "No work is fine. Actually, I am having issues with the mother of my kids. We had an argument when I brought the kids home from school." He scratched his head. "I don't know if you want to hear about it."

"Of course, if you want to talk about it."

"We lived together for four years. We have the kids together but ..." He paused and shifted uncomfortably in the chair. "Things are just not working out. I stayed around even though I couldn't do anything right or make her happy. But I can't do it anymore." He sighed. "So, I moved out two weeks ago. I'm living alone now so her new complaint is that I'm being selfish."

"I am sorry." Elisa felt bad that he was troubled but inside she felt a guilty joy that he was alone.

"No, please don't worry about me." He got up quickly. "I've said too much and I must go." He paused with his hand on the door. "Can I ask you something?"

"Sure."

"Would you like to go for a walk at the Parque

Municipal on Sunday? We can talk about more pleasant things and there is a zoo with alligators, jaguars, harpy eagles, and snakes. A botanical garden, too."

"I would love that." "But you know I grew up in a jungle with wild animals just a heartbeat away from my tambo. Lovely orchids draped from the trees. Jaguars slinked around in the dark, and snakes sometimes wound around the roof beams." His eyes opened so wide that she laughed. "But let's go. I'll tell you some funny stories."

"Well, then. I'll see you on Sunday." He seemed more relaxed as he closed the door behind him.

"And I will see you on Sunday." *In four days*, she sang to herself. Then she realized in a moment of panic: "I don't have really anything to wear on Sunday."

The next afternoon Elisa asked, "Marty. Can I leave early today?"

"Of course, why? What's wrong?"

"Candelario invited me for a walk Sunday. I just want to get a dress before the shop closes."

"Oh. that. I notice my brother is around a lot. He is a good guy. He broke up with his wife Delila. Perhaps you noticed," she said sarcastically, "he is in his twenties and you are fourteen, Elisa. I am not your mother, but I just want you to be careful. I don't want you to get hurt."

Marty made her feel like a child. Elisa's mind grumbled. Everyone keeps telling me to be careful. I'm here, basically on my own, taking care of myself. Can somebody be happy for me?

"I'll come back an hour earlier tomorrow."

Marty turned back to the sewing machine and drawled, "Ahllll right, young woman. See you tomorrow." Elisa picked up her purse and walked out the door in a huff.

There was a group of nice shops about a ten-minute walk from Marty's. Elisa entered one of the stores Prudencia had taken her to when she first moved to the city. Only eight months ago! She had plenty of time. She wandered through the store and held up several dresses: floral prints, bright colors, floor-length, knee-high. Nothing grabbed her attention until she picked up a white sundress from a pile of dresses in a sale bin. The tag said ten balboa.

"Perfect and I can actually afford to buy sandals, too," she whispered, then asked a sales woman. "Where do you have the sandals?"

"I'll show you. Nice dress you picked. White will show off your lovely complexion. I could never figure why no one bought it. It must have been waiting just for you. Are you looking for something to go with it?"

"Shoes for a walk in the Parque Municipal."

"Ah, with a sweetheart, no doubt."

Elisa blushed.

The sales woman chuckled. "Sit here. I have some new sandals that aren't even on display yet, just arrived yesterday." She disappeared behind a curtain then came back with the box. "Here, these are size five and a half. Try them on."

Elisa slipped them on and walked up and down the aisle. They fit perfectly. "I love them."

"The lavender color with the white flowers complement the dress, and ankle straps on top are in fashion this summer."

"Do you think that the straps will cause blisters?"

"No, no at all."

"Okay, I like that the heals are low and the toes are exposed. They are comfortable." Elisa grinned. "I'll take them. Thank you so much.

The sales woman winked at her. "Have fun!"

At the cash register Elisa saw a basket of different colored nail polish and little bottles of nail polish remover. She saw one with the same lavender color as the sandals.

She placed her dress and shoes on the counter and said, "I will take this lavender nail polish, too."

It was dark when she left the store. The employees of

some shops were pulling down the front doors to close for the day. Elisa felt like such a city woman as she walked back up the hill to Juana's place. Is he really my sweetheart? she wondered. I'm going to see him soon. That's what matters most.

Juana and Roberto were at church when Candelario knocked on the door.

His eyes lit up when he saw her. "You look great," he said immediately. "What a sweet dress."

"Yes, it's really pretty, isn't it? I loved it as soon as I saw it."

He laughed. "That's what I like about you. So honest and real." He handled her a bouquet of lavender flowers. "This is for you."

"Oh, thank you. I love them. They match my sandals! And smell so nice. I am going to put them in water."

"I'll wait for you out here."

Elisa rushed to the kitchen, found a vase, and ran to her bedroom. She placed the flowers on her night stand knowing she would be so pleased to sleep with them next to her tonight. She inhaled the lavender's scent and slowed down her excited heart.

Candelario held her hand as they walked to the park. Elisa felt the sun warm her skin. Her hand was moist in his but she didn't mind.

"So, you haven't said much." Candelario broke the silence. "You've been six months here in the city ...."

"Eight." I corrected him. "I like it a lot. Life in the village was one job after another. Picking plants, preparing them, making baskets, caring for children …Life here seems easier. I mean I work but life is my own. I walk to work, I'm learning so much from Marty …" She looked up at him with wide eyes. "I have you in my life. You make me happy."

"And you make me happy," said Candelario. "I think about you every day. I … I wish my circumstances were different."

He thinks about me every day! She squeezed his hand. "We can work it out. I know you have two kids. We both are busy. It's okay."

"You are fourteen, Elisa. I will have to wait until you are eighteen before we really ... What am I doing?" Candelario put his free hand to his forehead.

Elisa thought of the warnings of Ninfa, Prudencia, and Marty. Even Juana. "Nobody needs to know. I just want to be with you."

He put his arm around her waist. "Me too. You are such a sweet girl."

An ice cream truck passed by ringing a bell. He read her mind. "Do you want some ice cream?"

Elisa giggled. "Yes, I do."

"Anything for you!" He flagged the truck and bought her two scoops of fresh chocolate ice cream.

Three months passed. "The rainy season is back," said Juana over lunch.

"This is Panama. It rains every day. Why are you surprised?" asked Roberto with a laugh.

"Well, we're going to church anyway."

After they ate, Elisa went to the kitchen to do dishes. Juana picked up her purse and gazed at her. "Are you coming to church with us?"

"No, I am going to stay home. Candelario invited me to the movies today."

"Alright, we better get going before it starts raining," said Robert. "It's going to pour. From the heavens!"

I sat on the sofa waiting for Candelario. I get to see Candelario again. Every Sunday my sweetheart invites me to do something. She loved the word *sweetheart*. She heard the rain pummeling the roof wondering if he might not make it today. "The news ... Let me see what they say about the weather." Elisa turned on the radio and heard the announcer talking about this big storm hitting the coast. The first thing that came to her mind was Prudencia. "I hope the kiosko holds together this time."

She wanted to call her but Juana didn't have telephone service and it was usually the first thing to go out in this kind of weather anyway. "I am praying for you, my friend Prudencia."

Candelario was obviously going to be late. To distract herself, Elisa decided to do some chores around the house for Juana. She did laundry, cooked some rice for their dinner, and cleaned the shower. All the while hoping to see Candelario. After folding the second load of Juana's clothes, she decided to take a nap on her pink bed. Listening to rain and ferocious winds against the window, she closed her eyes...

Abruptly she reopened her eyes. It was almost dark outside. What time is it? she wondered sleepily. Then she heard something pounding on the door. It took a minute for her to realize it wasn't the storm. She swung her legs off the bed, ran to the front door, and flung it open. It was pouring outside. The street had turned into a river of brown water. Candelario was in a dark corner of the porch wearing a soaked yellow poncho.

"Candelario, come on, please. Get in here." She tried to close the door behind him but the wind wouldn't let her. They pulled it shut together. Then paused to look at each other. She was rumpled and he was dripping rainwater from his poncho. His hair was plastered to his head.

"I am sorry; I fell asleep."

"Don't worry. We're not going to be able to go anywhere. The streets are completely flooded."

"Oh, no. Juana isn't here. They left for church hours ago."

"They're fine. The church is in a high elevation. They are probably worrying about you right now. There is no way for them to get here or contact you, Elisa. There's a power outage."

She ran to the wall to turn the light switch on and off several times while looking at the small ceiling chandelier. "Yep, it's not working. I have to look for some candles and get you a towel. Wow are you wet." She went to the bathroom to grab a towel for him. "Candelario, come here and put the poncho in the bathtub."

He took his boots and the poncho off and placed them in the tub to dry off. "Here is the towel." He turned around. His body was close to hers, his shirt damp and warm. He grabbed her by her neck gently and pulled her toward his lips. He kissed Elisa passionately. She trembled, dropped the towel, and welcomed his kisses. The night was young, they were alone, and she let her desire for him take over with joy. She lost herself to him.

The rain stopped at some point in the night. Elisa didn't want it to end. Candelario was in her bed, under the blankets with her, sleeping quietly. She lay her head on his chest and used his body as a long pillow. She was sore and her inner thighs were numb from their lovemaking. Even though she had lost her virginity to him, she didn't feel it was a loss but a gain. A gain of being so close to the man she loved. She was wide awake in a state of complete certainty, thinking over and over: I know he will be with me forever.

Then she came to her senses. She sat up and listened. "It's stopped raining." She listened again. "Oh no, Juana is going to come home soon."

Candelario opened his eyes and looked around the room as if he didn't know where he was. Then he pulled her back under the covers and held her tight. He kissed her tenderly then whispered, "Thank you for this amazing moment."

Elisa smiled, in heaven again with his love.

"Do you want me to leave?"

She frowned. "I don't … but I don't want Juana to find you here."

"Okay, I'll see you next Sunday." He got dressed quickly. It felt strange to be so ordinarily friendly as she walked him to the front door. "Oh wait! Your poncho."

She ran to the bathtub and picked it up. It was still wet. She grabbed the towel that was still on the floor from last night and quickly wiped it dry. She couldn't do much for the shoes.

He stood in the doorway and grinned at her. "Relax, sweetheart." She stared at him. He said it! I am his sweetheart. "There's still a lot of water in the street. Don't go to work. I'll talk to Marty when I go to check on her. Stay home." He kissed me. "We made our own storm, didn't we?" Then he left.

As Elisa closed the door, a sense of guilt came over her, and she pondered, Why am I feeling this way? If what happened was pure and beautiful? The numbness of her thighs was gone. She felt weightless, like walking on air.

Despite the storm, the work weeks didn't slow down. They got new customers and Elisa measured them herself. She opened the files and entered the measurements in each new binder.

But she hadn't heard from Candelario since their glorious night together. Today the phone had rung off the hook all day and it rang again. But she left that to Marty and took care of the current customer in the fitting area "Alright, you are all set, sir. Your pair of pants should be done by next Friday."

"Thank you. You're great, Elisa. So quick and easy."

She folded the two colors of fabric he had chosen and added them to the stack of material in the closet with the rest of the new projects. Each one had a delivery day and name on a piece of paper pinned to the fabric. "I'll show you the way out, Mr. Madero."

The phone rang again as she walked him to the front door, but Marty didn't call her. Today is Friday and Candelario still hasn't called. She felt a little nervous but tried to be optimistic. Maybe he's busy. He'll call later. She'd been saying this to herself for days.

She helped Marty put things away before she left for

the day. "Do you want me to help you with anything else?"

"No, Elisa. You've helped me a lot. It's been a crazy week!""

"It sure has. I'll be ready for more on Monday. See you then."

"Have a good weekend, Elisa." Then Marty looked up and said. "You probably already know this, but my brother Candelario is back with his wife … again. We'll see how long it lasts this time."

Elisa walked home in shock, feeling so sad and wondering how he could say in one minute that she was his sweetheart and in the next go back to his wife who argued with him. As she opened the door to Juana's living room, their phone was ringing. Maybe this is Candelario! Maybe he'll explain. Elisa ran to the phone. "Hello?"

"Hi Elisa. It's Prudencia."

"Is everything okay?"

"Yes, everything is fine. I was just wondering if you could help us build the extension of our porch at the kiosko and help replace the roof with stronger materials."

"When?"

"This weekend? I know its short notice …"

"Yes, of course," Elisa said without hesitation. Elisa was always happy to help Prudencia she had helped her so much. She was happy her friend reached out to her. I miss the twins, her food. "I'll catch the bus and meet you there tomorrow. Gladly." She also wanted to run from her heartbreak. What better way to forget.

"Bring clothes. Spend the whole weekend. It'll be fun."

With overnight clothes in her handbag, Elisa rode the bus to Concepción. It was Saturday, very early, so there weren't many people, only about six. The driver still played the music at full blast, though.

At her stop the driver braked and opened the door with the manual lever. She stepped down and got a clear view of PRUDENCIA'S awning above the kiosko. There were several people eating.

"Elisa is here!" Antonio yelled. The twins ran to bear hug her.

"You are growing so much, boys!"

"Yes, it's our birthday today."

"Oh, I wish I'd known. So, who is older?"

"I am," said Antonio.

Marcelo pushed him. "By what? Two minutes? Please!"

"Happy Birthday to both of you!"

Prudencia waited for me at the counter with a warm smile. I didn't know how much I missed them until then.

"Well. You look good. I love your new fashion," said Prudencia. "and your haircut to your shoulders."

"Thank you. It's easy to buy clothes now that I live close to the stores. I walk ten minutes and I am right there."

"Well, you look happy," said Prudencia.

"I really like my work."

She hugged Elisa. "You deserve all good things."

Elisa hugged her back and didn't want to let go.

Of course Prudencia wanted to feed her. "We already ate breakfast. So, I'll make you something and sit with you to catch up before we start working." They walked passed the new helpers. "So, the twins, you, and Rudy are helping but who are the rest of these guys?"

"They are the construction crew. They have plenty of experience. They are experts. We're here to help *accelerate* the process," she whispered. "Otherwise they take long lunch breaks."

"Ah, to save money." Elisa said. "I am sure they are charging you a lot." Everything was dirty and in the construction mode. Prudencia led her to a table that was pushed in the corner.

"Wait here. I will bring you a chicken empanada and

coffee."

A crew member came over. "Are you ready to work? Hi. I'm Omar." She extended her hand to shake his. "Oh no, my hands are too dirty, sorry."

"It's fine. I'll be dirty pretty soon, too." She shook his black hand covered with dust from the dry concrete. She felt his calluses. "I am Elisa."

Prudencia brought coffee and put it on the table.

"Well. I will let you both eat." Omar backed away, although he looked at that cup of coffee longingly.

"We will be there shortly, Omar," said Prudencia firmly.

And soon enough, the hammering and lifting and mixing … and a share of grumbling and cursing … began for the renovation of Prudencia's building.

The next day, Elisa felt a little lightheaded as they worked at the kiosko again. "The wall is finished," said Omar. "But we have to wait at least two hours for the cement mix to dry up between the blocks."

"Okay. It's time to eat lunch anyways," said Prudencia. "Can you help me, Elisa?"

Inside the kitchen she wondered. "I see you are a little distant. Are you okay?"

"I'm not feeling perfect. Maybe it's the heat."

She felt her coffee rise up. Elisa patted her chest a couple of times to see if that helped, and it did a little bit.

"Have a seat, Elisa. You're pale as a ghost," said Prudencia, pulling out a chair for her.

Instead she ran to the alley behind the restaurant and threw up all over. Elisa felt surprisingly better after that, rinsed her hands in the outdoor faucet, wiped her face with the cool water, and drank some, too. But it smelled like coins and she nearly threw up again. She took a few deep breaths and went back in the kitchen.

"Are you feeling better?"

"Yes, much better … for some reason I am very sensitive to smells lately."

Prudencia's face went still as stone. "Well, if you were with somebody sexually, I would say that you're pregnant."

She took a deep breath so Prudencia wouldn't notice her expression. Her heart nearly thumped out of her chest with fear. "I think I'll eat later."

"Alright, hon," Prudencia said softly and turned away. "Marcelo and Antonio let's eat!" she yelled, just like she always did. That made Elisa so happy.

When the weekend was over, work ruled her day as usual. The nausea in the morning persisted ... and what Prudencia said on Sunday weekend nagged at Elisa's mind. And then she didn't menstruate as usual. She was fearfully doubtful. I only had sex one time ... Could I really be pregnant?

Candelario didn't show up again the following Sunday. She decided she had to find out if she was in trouble, and there was only one way she knew how to do that. In the middle of the next week, Elisa left Marty's house as usual but instead of walking to Juana's, she went down the hill and yelled "Taxi!"

It pulled over and she got in.

"Where to, lady?"

"Take me to the nearest clinic."

Elisa sat in the lobby of the private clinic waiting for somebody to call her name. The smell of medicine and the chilly air conditioning made her uncomfortable and nostalgic for the aromatic heat of the jungle. She almost dozed off thinking of the clear stream that ran next to the village.

A nurse came for her fifteen minutes after she signed in. "Elisa Carama?"

"Yes." She was glad she had shortened her name from Cheucarama. She didn't want any curious questions about her origins. Carama sounded more Panamanian and less Chocó.

"Come with me." He smiled without looking in her eyes. It was a nice smile but not deep. "How are you today?"

"I am worried."

"I see that you are here to get a pregnancy test."

"Yes." She followed him into an examining room. It was first time she had ever been in a medical clinic. It was very white.

"Okay. Just have a seat and I'll get a small sample of blood from your arm." He patted a vein in her arm a couple of times until it was visible. "It won't hurt."

He inserted the needle in her forearm. It felt like it went straight to her bone and she winced.

"Well, maybe a little."

"More than a little!"

"Sorry. The results should be ready in an hour. You can sit in the lobby until then."

She sat and waited, staring at the wall clock. The hands moved so slowly. She was shivering in that phony cold air that almost hurt her skin. Her thoughts drifted back home again. I wish Ninfa was here. Elisa almost wept at the thought. She always knew what to do, or what to say to make her feel better, or she didn't have to say anything, just her presence was enough. Elisa thought about how her desire to go to school vanished when she met Candelario. He had possessed her thoughts and now he didn't even call. How had that happened? Everything all the wise women in her life had warned her about had come true. Prayers seemed her best path at the moment: Please God help me. If the results are negatives, I will follow my dreams. I will get back on track.

"Elisa, the results are ready." The nurse waved at her to follow him.

She looked at the clock. Only forty-five minutes has passed. She walked into the same white room he had taken her for the test. He handed her a piece of paper. "This is the result."

She grabbed the pink paper from him and read the

results. "Are you sure?"

"Yes, Elisa. It's positive. I'm sorry."

She stared at it in silence.

"Would you like to make an appointment with the doctor … about how to take care of yourself during pregnancy?"

"Uh, not today. Soon, though."

"Well, there are certain ways to take care …" and the nurse droned on with information she simply couldn't take in.

Soon she walked out of the clinic in a daze. "I don't know what to do now," she whispered to the evening light.

A taxi honked. "Do you need a taxi?"

Elisa nodded and climbed in. "Central Ave. Please."

She got home to no one. Juana wasn't there or Robert. She went to her pretty bedroom still holding the pink paper that matched the bedspread and the curtains and the walls. Suddenly, she cried and cried, unable to stop.

"Elisa, are you okay?"

She realized too late she had forgotten to close the door.

"Can I come in?"

Elisa couldn't talk so she just nodded. She took a shirt from a pile of laundry on her bed and buried her face in the soft cotton fabric.

"What's wrong?"

She handed the pink paper to Juana.

"What's this?" She read it. "Is this a pregnancy test? Oh my, it's positive." She sat next to Elisa, pulled the shirt from her face, Elisa saw that Juana's her face was mysteriously full of joy.

"But I don't want …"

"Oh, my dear, this is a blessing to my house, Elisa. Don't be sad. You are blessed."

"I don't know what to do? Candelario returned to his ex and I don't have anybody."

Juana hugged her tight. "You have me. I wanted a child, you know? But I guess I wasn't meant to carry one. But I prayed ... Oh, I prayed to have one in this house. I imagined listening to the little fat toddler feet stomping around my floor." She laughed. "I will help you, Elisa. You are not alone. My heart is filled with joy and yours will be, too."

"I am not ready for this. I don't know how to be a mother."

"It is okay, sweet woman. It's natural that you're scared and confused. You are very young. Your love will grow as your child grows inside of you."

Everything pouring out of Juana was soothing, loving, and reassuring. Her words and embraces were the right medicine for Elisa's soul.

Chapter 7
You're an Indian

Elisa went to the public clinic to see a doctor for the first time. She had to stand up in the lobby because there weren't enough seats, but she didn't mind, although she was glad she was close to the door. The four fans on the ceiling weren't enough ventilation for the number of people in the room. She felt nauseated from the smell of the fried food some snacked on as they waited. "Oh, please, God, help me get through this." And as if He had heard her, the next name called was hers.

"Elisa Carama. This way please." The nurse had a white dress that fell right below her knees. Why did I notice that? Elisa shook her head; pregnancy made her think odd thoughts and want to eat odd food, like naranjillas, fried yucca, and especially Juana's temptation plantains.

"I'm Nurse Clara. How are is your pregnancy going?" She adjusted her strange nurse's hat. Elisa was glad this was not her own profession of choice, if only because she didn't like the uniform.

"Oh, I'm not sure."

"That's okay. We will help you find out. Let's take your blood sample."

"Again? You already know I'm pregnant."

The nurse chuckled. "Oh, blood tells us a lot more than that. Sit here."

Elisa knew what to expect this time and extended her arm, preparing for the bone-piercing pain. The nurse tied the robber string around her biceps and tapped the place to find a vein.

"When was your last menstruation?" Nurse Clara asked as she inserted the needle.

"Eight weeks ago. Sheesh!" Elisa answered with a wince.

"All done, now let me get your blood pressure." The nurse put a little circular bandage on the dot of blood from the needle and on her other arm wrapped a black belt-like strap with a pump attached to it, pumping it up until her arm felt like a balloon.

"Is the father here with you?"

"He's at work right now." Elisa didn't want to reveal her private life. The tight belt began to loosen slowly.

"Alright, the doctor will be here soon." She grabbed her notes and put them in a folder that had Elisa's name on it, left it on a counter, and closed the door behind her. She looked at the posters around the room. One showed a figure of a pregnant woman. You could see the baby's form already through an X-ray.

Elisa held herself. "There is a baby inside of me," she whispered.

After a knock at the door, man with a white jacket came in. "Hello, Elisa. I am Dr. Rangel." He shook her sweaty hand.

"Hi," she said shyly.

He took the folder from the counter and opened it. After reading it quickly he sat and faced her. "Are you excited to be a mom for the first time?" His voice was kind.

Elisa shook her head. For some reason, she didn't want to lie to him.

"I understand." He glanced at the chart again. "You're about fourteen years old. I can't imagine …"

"I might be fifteen," she interrupted. "I was born in a small village in the Darién where my people didn't exactly keep track of birth dates. All I know is I was born in the summer."

He looked at her face with great curiosity, began to ask her something, but stopped himself. Instead he asked, "You lived in the jungle." She nodded. "Have you ever had malaria?"

"What?"

"Um, a disease where you get high fever and many die of it."

"Never."

"Have you ever had tuberculosis?"

"What?"

"Um, an illness with lots of coughing, even coughing up blood. It doesn't go away by itself."

"No. My people rarely got sick. Like I said, when they did, the healer Jaibana took care of them."

"So do you know if any of the women in your family had any problems with childbirth?"

"No. Never. All the babies were born just fine. Jaibana and women helped. He would prepare a special plant and they would attend …"

The doctor shrugged and cut in. "Ah yes. The village healer and midwives." He wrote something in the chart again. "Do you have family here? I think there are many Chocó people. But in Panama City they are often poor. Not well."

Elisa paused. She hadn't seen many native people like her except occasionally mixed in with everybody else. She had the sense that the doctor might try to change her situation if he thought she was poor. She thought of Juana. "Yes. I have good family. Not poor."

"Okay, I was just saying that I can't imagine how scary this must be for you ... being so young … but I promise we'll make sure that the whole pregnancy is safe. We will watch you and the baby like a hawk to make sure that you both stay healthy. Could you bring in a family member next time you come, please? Okay?" She nodded. He touched her arm and smiled. "Now back to your history. Alright, so what we have here? It said that the last period you had was eight weeks ago. Hmm. Do you remember when you had the last sexual encounter?"

"Yes, six weeks ago."

"Alright, so looking at the calculation chart, your baby will be born next year, February 20, 1949. Or a week or so on either side of that date would still be normal. Here is a prescription for you to pick up in the lobby. The counter on the left at the end of the hall. It's your daily vitamins. The nurse will give you your next appointment." Dr. Rangel closed the folder. "Is there anything else?"

"No."

"So I will see you next month, Elisa." He left the room and she left a moment later, walking straight down the hall to the counter with a little hole in a long window.

"I'm here to pick up my vitamins." She handed the blue paper to the clerk.

"Elisa Carama?"

"Yes."

"I have it right here for you along with your next appointment time." She handed her a little white bag with a time/date card attached.

"Thank you. Where do I pay?"

The woman looked at the chart. "Oh, you don't have to pay. You're an Indian."

That puzzled Elisa. "Why does that make a difference?"

The woman rolled her eyes. "The government is trying to figure out what to do with you all."

Elisa left the clinic puzzled by that comment but relieved that at least she had the date of birth. She clutched the small white bag with the vitamins inside. It was midmorning, and she was already late for work. She swallowed hard, "Well, I have to tell Marty sooner or later." Ninfa came to mind. Elisa held the crucifix on the gold chain. "I will have to tell her, too. She'll probably be happy about it."

Five weeks after Elisa's last visit to the doctor she still hadn't found a way to tell Marty.

"It's almost lunch time," Marty said after a morning of stocking the shelves with new bolts of material. "I think I am going to order some Chinese food. What do you want?"

"I'm not hungry." Elisa continued cutting a pattern for pants.

"How can you weigh so much if you're not eating?" Marty said this with a smirk. "Unless you're pregnant." She looked in my eyes as waiting for me to confirm.

I stopped cutting and put the scissors down. I sighed. "Yes, I am pregnant."

"I knew it!" Marty walked to the phone. "I am still going to order some food and you are going to eat ... Then, I want to hear all about it."

After the food arrived they sat at the table to eat, but Elisa still wasn't hungry. Her so-called morning sickness wasn't only in the morning; it came without warning.

"I'm just going to eat the soup."

"Okay, hon. As long as you eat something. Let me just ask you. Is Candelario the father?"

Elisa stared at the soup and whispered, "Yes ... yes, he is ... but I don't want to tell him."

"But why not?"

She sipped just a spoonful of soup. It was nice and warm, sort of like a blessing. "I don't want him to think that I got pregnant just to keep him around." She answered as calmly as possible. It hurt just to think of him. But it was the truth. "Also, he doesn't care about me anymore. I haven't seen him since ..."

"I think he deserves to know," said Marty forcefully. "He might be kind of a jerk about women, but he is a good father. I don't know about a good husband, but he does take good care of his kids."

Elisa thought about this. "I guess I'd tell him if I knew how to get in touch with him."

"I'll give you his phone number and then you can call him."

"Okay." She trembled with fear at the thought of hearing his voice. She didn't want to call him. She felt like she had enough trouble with the morning sickness and her unhappiness. She didn't like lying to Marty, but she also didn't really think it was Marty's place to tell her to call the man who had left her without so much as a wave. I won't call him ... at least not yet.

After work Elisa went for a walk down Central Ave. Her skirts and blouses were getting tight. She had noticed a store around the corner conveniently called EVA'S ROPA DE MATERNIDAD. She stood outside the display window and gazed at the mannequins with well-formed bellies. "I can't imagine I'll look like that when I get big. All skinny and fabulous," Elisa muttered.

"Hi dear." An older woman came to the door. "Looking for a gift?"

Maybe she knows I'm embarrassed to say it's for me. "Y … Yes, for a friend of mine."

She grinned with a twinkle in her eye. "That's thoughtful. How far is she into her *embarazo*?"

"She just started. A couple of months. Are you Eva?"

"I am."

"I have a friend with a food kiosko in Concepción that is named after herself. PRUDENCIA'S. It feels more like family to eat there and most everyone is a regular." Elisa furrowed her brow. Why am I so chatty? More weirdness of my embarazo, I guess.

"I totally agree," said Eva. "I can be like a good friend because most girls … like your friend, no doubt … are uncomfortable with their growing bodies. I'll show you the one-size fits all skirts. She'll be able to use it from now to the end." She grabbed one from the shelf and showed me. "See … stretches right here in the middle and doesn't have elastic because that will make the skin itch—and she doesn't want to scratch her belly, trust me."

"So, how does it stretch there?"

"Drawstring." Eva pulled the two ends of ribbon that ran through the waistband of the skirt. The waistline tightened. Then she loosened them and the waistline stretched. "Just like that. Simple."

"Clever. I'll take three of those. In solid colors. The yellow and a red. Oh and that pretty turquoise blue."

Eva folded the skirts into a silver bag. "It will be fifteen balboas for each dress. Total is forty-five plus the crazy government taxes. But I'll give you a nice discount. Just forty. I hope you … and your friend … come back."

Elisa took the cash from my purse and gave her the money.

"Anything else, hon?"

"No, you've been really helpful. I'll … I mean we'll … certainly be back."

"Have a good evening and good luck with your new baby." Eva winked at Elisa playfully.

Elisa smiled back. That felt better than trying to pretend.

Walking home, she stopped at an ice cream wagon for some ice cream she'd been craving. In line behind three people she thought about all the flavors on the list, salivating at the possibilities. Finally she got to the window.

"Hi Elisa. What can I get you today?"

The owners knew her well. She was a regular.

"Hi, Tomás. Can I have a cherry ice cream in a large cup? I love the color. And it tastes like the real fruit."

He laughed. "It is the real fruit! And now that you are eating for two, young lady, you must treat yourself to the best. How far along are you? I can see that round belly now."

"Seventeen and a half weeks."

"Here it is. One balboa."

I handed him the bill. "Well ... don't work too hard. Baby comes first."

"I wish, but I have no choice but to work hard."

"Anyway, have a good evening."

She ambled up the hill to Juana's enjoying ice cream as if she hadn't had it in years—instead of just two days. It was gone by the time she got to the front door. "So good!" She smacked her chilly lips. Who knew ice cream could make you this happy, at least for a minute.

She fished out her key from the bottom of her purse,

the silver bag over her arm. She opened the door and heard voices coming from the dining table. She recognized Juana's but not the other females. Elisa dropped her things on the small sofa with yellow flowers and walked toward them.

"Hi." Elisa smiled in greeting. Any friend of Juana's would undoubtedly be someone she'd like too.

The both looked at her in silence.

Juana finally cleared her throat. "Hi, Elisa. Come have a seat." After she sat and put her elbows on the table, waiting for the mysterious person to be introduced, Juana added, "This is Delila, Candelario's wife."

"Hi." Elisa tried not to show her utter shock. She wanted to run from the table, but she was frozen. Delila was a beautiful woman. She had the same skin complexion as Juana and her hair was styled straight back, although some breakaway strands revealed it was naturally very curly hair. Confusion overcame her. Why did I notice another silly detail? As if I'm not sitting here facing Candelario's wife?

Delila lifted her chin. "You are probably wondering why I'm here."

"Yes, of course I am."

Juana stood up. "Well, I am going to let you two talk. I have to finish some laundry. Let me know if you need anything."

Juana walked away and there they were: Candelario's one-time girlfriend with Candelario's wife.

"So, what do you want?" Elisa asked this question as quietly as possible.

Delila looked straight into her eyes. "I want you to stay away from my husband."

"What are you talking about?" Elisa kept calm even though her heart raced.

"I know about you and Candelario."

"So, what do you know?"

"Marty called Candelario to let him know about your pregnancy."

Elisa fell back onto the chair. "I can't believe she did that?"

"Candelario talked to me last night and told me everything."

"Oh yeah ... everything?" Elisa felt betrayed. "Did he tell you that he was the one who was after me?" Then she was completely angry. "Taking me out on dates and telling me that you two broke up and he had moved out. He 'couldn't do it' were his words about your marriage ... I hope he told you that part!"

"We did break up. But we are back together now." Delila haughtily brushed back one of her break-away curls. "However, we are honorable people ..." Elisa scoffed at that. "He'll certainly take care of the baby. He *wants* to take care of the baby. I told him that was fine. I will even help. I just don't want him to ever see *you* again." She looked away as if disturbed about that possibility.

"Really!? A man that doesn't show his face to accept a mess he created, is a man that is not worth seeing again ... Tell him that, because you obviously have no pride."

"I am the mother of his children. One makes sacrifices."

They sat in dark silence.

Delila began again. "When the baby is old enough, I will come and get him for a few hours for Candelario to see him ... or her."

"You don't rule my life, either of you. I don't care about what you want or don't want. I am the mother of *this* child. I decide. Get out."

To Elisa's surprise, Delila got up out of the chair, walked stiffly toward the door, and left. She stared blankly at the space where the woman had been sitting just seconds before.

Juana returned from laundry room. "I overheard everything. Are you okay, Elisa?"

"This is nightmare. Now he wants to take the child."

"You really stood up for yourself." Juana sat next to

her and rubbed her hand on the young woman's back "I know, Elisa. This is a difficult situation," she said and drew in a breath. "But in my opinion, I think it is good for the baby if the father is involved, for financial reasons as well as for the baby. You can set the terms, the times and days."

"I hate him." Elisa cried out in a fury. "I hate myself."

"Try not to get so upset, Elisa. This is not good for the baby. I'll tell you what. I'll make you green tea and a grilled sandwich for dinner. I know you'll like that."

Elisa sat at the table sobbing like a little girl. She let out everything that had been bottled up for so long. Aching for the cowardly Candelario. Then understanding he was worthless. Never wanting but now loving the child inside her womb.

Next day, she got up to go to work. She really didn't want to, but she needed to ask Marty why she spoke to Candelario. And ask who gave her that right? Elisa needed an explanation. Who was her friend and who was not?

She opened the door with the key Marty had made for her. She walked straight to the workshop. She immediately blurted out, "Why did you tell Candelario about me being pregnant," straight to the point.

"Excuse me! Why are you yelling at me in my house, young lady?" Martina fired back. "Let me just tell you something," she rose up from her sewing machine, "Candelario is my brother. We are family. You didn't tell him about your pregnancy when you said you would. Remember you promised. The baby is growing inside of you. Somebody needed to make a grownup decision."

"Delila came to my house to talk to me, with no warning," Elisa said. "And I thought you and I were friends. I feel betrayed from every angle. He is a horrible person, you must admit, a coward for not facing me himself. I am fourteen, what did I know? He hung around to charm me, call me his sweetheart, complain about his wife. Then, conveniently he went back with Delila. He is a cold, dishonest, calculating man."

"You are talking about my brother? He helped you find a job and cared for you. How ungrateful you are, *india*. Get out of my house now!"

"Indian? This is not about where I was born. This is not about work. I've done a good job for you …"

"Shut up!" Marty grabbed my hair and pulled me to the door. "I've had it with you. I don't want to see you again. You whore!" She pushed the girl onto the porch, slammed the door behind her, and clanked the latch angrily on the inside. Elisa was locked out.

But she wiped the tears fiercely from her eyes while standing out in the street. She walked slowly back to Juana's house. Now without a job and a baby on the way. She held her belly as if already holding the child in her arms.

Elisa spent all day crying in the pink bedroom. All her dreams had been torn apart by her ignorance of how cruel people could be. "How can I ever recover from this?" She sobbed and then slept in between cries until she heard a gentle knock at the door.

"Elisa, are you awake?"

"Come in, Juana." She sat up in bed and tried to comb her hair with her fingers.

"I've been worried all day about you at work because I heard you crying last night. Did you go to work today?"

"I did ... but Marty fired me."

"She what?!"

I felt Juana's sympathy. It helped me open up more. "She called me indian and whore. Candelario had only been helping me and I was ungrateful and stupid. She yanked me by my hair and pushed me out the door."

"That is unacceptable." Juana was shaking. "Do you want me to talk to her?"

"No! ... Please." Juana was a kind and gentle person. Elisa couldn't drag her into a nasty argument. Besides, her husband Roberto would get involved too and the whole situation was already embarrassing and humiliating.

"I did talk poorly of her brother."

"That doesn't give her any right to mistreat you or insult you."

"I don't worry about that. I deserve it for being so stupid."

"You are not stupid, Elisa. You are courageous by coming to this city all by yourself. He was a mistake that brought you a blessing. See it that way, please," Juana begged.

Elisa sighed. "I just need to find a new job. I have enough saved for the rent and the food for the next three months, but I need to start to look for jobs tomorrow."

"You are already five and a half months, Elisa. It will be hard for you to get a job. Companies don't hire pregnant women."

"I know ... I'll try anyway."

"If you can't find a job, it's okay. Roberto and I make enough to support you until the baby is born. We have done it all alone before you came to live with us. Promise me you won't become fearful. You have us."

"Okay." She grabbed Juana's hand. She was the steady rock Elisa needed now. She was her angel.

After three weeks of applying for new jobs, she couldn't find anything. They all asked for pregnancy test and a picture along with the form. The walking in to shops with HELP WANTED signs on the door didn't hire her either as her belly was getting bigger. She got dressed one Monday morning ... not to look for jobs but to visit the doctor for a check-up. Elisa took the bus this time instead of a taxi, needing to save as much as possible. She brought fried bread that Juana made for breakfast in a brown paper bag just in case hunger struck, as it so often did.

The bus was empty. It was early in the morning but late enough that most had already gone to their jobs. The old bus went fast since it didn't have a lot of stops. After only twenty minutes, the driver stopped at the hospital entrance. Since she was early, Elisa got off the bus and walked around the area open to the public. It was a nice walk. This sun was made her feel warm and energetic. Morning sickness didn't happen as often; she felt more like herself this morning. While walking, Elisa felt something shift inside. She kept walking with a hand on the side of her big belly. And there it was! A kick on her palm. Elisa laughed and talked to her baby. "It's a good thing I'm here at the hospital. I hope you're okay." She went in the main door and signed in. Within fifteen minutes she heard "Elisa Carama."

"That's me."

"Come this way, my darling. I'm Gloria." The nurse seemed the most genuinely pleasant one of all her visits. She led Elisa to an examining room with a bed. "Have a seat here." She pulled some steps under the high bed and Elisa climbed up and sat down. After doing her regular blood pressure, pulse, and heart rate routine, Gloria told her, "Go ahead and lie down."

She pulled up Elisa's skirt. It was uncomfortable to feel so invaded, even by such a nice woman.

"I felt the baby kicking me today on the way here." Elisa smiled at the ceiling. "For the first time."

The nurse was carefully listening to her womb with a stethoscope. "The heart beat is healthy, too. All looks good." She placed her notes in the Elisa Carama folder, which was filled with paper now.

"I wish I knew what the baby's gender is."

"Yep. It would be nice. We can't do that yet, but it's part of the great mystery. First the heartbeat, then the kick, then the growth. Pretty soon it will turn around inside you. And finally you'll hear those wonderful words: It's a ....!" She chuckled. "Mystery solved." Elisa grinned at the thought. "Alright sit up now. The doctor will come in soon." Gloria patted her arm and walked out. Elisa thought, It's nice to know I'm part of a great mystery.

Elisa woke up from another hard kick. She was already eight and a half months along and rarely slept through the night. Juana joked that she was in training for taking care of the infant, who would rarely sleep through the night at first. Yet it made Elisa grumpy and short of breath. She was only comfortable on her side with pillows between her legs ... but not even that helped much anymore.

"It's dawn; I might as well just get up." She stretched and pushed her round unfamiliar body off the mattress. "I'll make breakfast for all of us."

Elisa went to the kitchen to grab a pot under the counter to make some eggs, but she couldn't even bend over. She knelt on the black and white tiled floor. Then strangely, she was certain she heard Juana crying softly. She struggled to stand up then waddled like a duck to the living room. Juana and Roberto were hugging each other. Over his shoulder Juana saw her watching.

Elisa backed away. "Oh, I'm sorry. I didn't mean to intrude but I heard Juana crying."

"It's okay." Roberto looked tired. "I'm on my way to work."

He kissed Juana. "Everything is going to be fine," he whispered softly.

Juana followed him and closed the door softly when he left.

"Juana, what's going on? Is everything okay?"

Juana sighed. She sat down on her little flowery sofa. She sighed again so deeply. "Roberto is dying. He has cancer."

Elisa gasped, sat beside her, and squeezed her hand.

"He has been fighting it for two years."

"I had no idea. He doesn't look sick. A little tired but he is so full of life."

"He is a strong man." Juana dropped her head on her hands. "If anything happens to him, I will be lost. He is my everything." She suddenly straightened up and looked at me. "I can't sit around or I'll fall apart. I don't want you to be affected by this bad news. It will hard on the baby. The little one will be our life, Elisa. Come on," she got up, "I'll take you out for breakfast."

They walked down to the coffee place on the corner. "It's kind of gloomy today." Elisa wrapped her sweater around her.

Juana looked up. "Rain is coming." Elisa stopped walking. "Are you okay?"

"I don't know."

Juana frowned. "What do you mean you don't know?"

"I feel fine. Just a little ..." Suddenly, Elisa felt warm liquid coming from between her legs. She couldn't control it. "Juana, Juana ... What is this?" She was terrified.

Juana was calm. "You broke your water. It means labor will start soon. We need to get to the hospital now. Stay here. I'll get a taxi," Juana stepped into the street and waved her arms.

Elisa stood in shock on the sidewalk. She remembered the nurse telling her something about this but not that it was so warm and so much. The water was running down the cracks in the bricks. Then a sharp pain passed over her lower abdomen and her legs trembled. Elisa groaned and sat down right on the sidewalk. She heard a door open from the house behind her.

"Oh my God ... A pregnant woman on the street!" a woman yelled. Elisa didn't even look up. All she could pay attention to was a pain that made her pant. "Bring a towel," the woman said to someone else. "Hon, you'll be fine. Just breathe deep."

The pain was suddenly gone. A soft rain began to fall and, strangely, it made Elisa feel calm. Juana pulled up in a red taxi. "Please, help me get her in." Juana begged. Two neighbors and the driver helped Elisa up. The woman spread the towel on the seat. "You can keep it."

When Elisa was settled in the taxi, Juana hopped in

beside her. "To Santo Tomás Hospital." It began to rain warmly and steadily as they drove across town.

Elisa sat in the familiar hospital lobby next to Juana, who was massaging her lower back. "That feels good. The pain is gone."

"You're in labor right now, hon. It will come back."

"I don't have my bag. I had everything ready; the diapers, baby clothes ... I didn't know it would be this way. So much I planned is useless now."

Juana laughed. "I know ... you packed and unpacked that bag dozens of times."

"Elisa Carama."

"Here, it's me."

"Come with me," the nurse ordered abruptly. Oh no. Elisa almost cried. One of the unfriendly ones.

"Hey, I was two hours before her," a black lady complained. "I'm going to deliver right here in the lobby. This is unbelievable. That kid got here ten minutes ago."

"She broke her water about forty minutes ago. We've got to get her ready," the nurse said.

Other women called out, "But I'm in pain!" "I need a bedpan!" "Help me!" Some women screamed even louder when they saw the nurse turn toward them.

"Stop screaming!" ordered the nurse. "This girl broke her waters. On the street for God sakes. Y'all haven't, so just sit down and BREATHE!"

Elisa and Juana followed her to the examining room. "Excuse me, you can't come to this room. It is only for pregnant women," she said to Juana. "You have to wait in the lobby."

"Okay." Juana nodded, although Elisa could hear her disappointment. "But I'll be out here waiting ...don't worry," she managed to say before the door completely closed.

"Lie down on this empty bed for now." The nurse pointed at a bed in the corner. There were three other women lying down in the room. "After one of these women deliver, then it's probably yer turn. No time to get in a dressing gown." She said this with an accent Elisa hadn't noticed before.

What if my baby comes before theirs? She thought and then spoke silently to herself: Trust the process, Elisa. That's what Juana would say.

While waiting, the lady in the next bed screamed in pain. Three nurses rushed in and spread her legs. "She's crowning. I see the head," one said. "Okay, dear, you have to push. It's all up to you now." The mother groaned and groaned; the nurses surrounded her saying, "Yes, come on. Here it comes!"

The male doctor walked in. "What do we have here?" he asked grabbing the chart.

"A delivery," said a nurse with obvious sarcasm.

The Elisa heard the baby cry. The doctor said. "It's a boy." That made her want to cry with joy herself, but she felt movements in her belly and suddenly another contraction took hold. The pain made her roll and moan.

One of the nurses came to her bed. "You're next, kiddo. We just have to clean the bed for you."

Elisa looked over at the new mother. She looked exhausted.

The nurse pulled back her sheet. "Here, open your legs. So, I can feel where your dilations are right now."

Elisa opened her legs and the nurse adjusted her knees up. She pulled her dress up. "Oh my gosh! Doctor ... we have to deliver right now. The head is visible. She has to push now." The doctor was examining the newborn. "Oh, I've got him," she said and took the infant from him. "Come and deliver this one."

The doctor came to her bed. He stood in between Elisa's knees. "Push," he insisted. He pulled the baby gently while Elisa pushed with all her might. "We're almost there."

Finally, she took a long last push and felt her infant enter the world. The doctor held it up but the baby was quiet. Elisa got scared. It didn't move. The doctor held the baby upside down and gave it a slap on the bottom. Elisa felt invaded and abused and vulnerable, unable to protect the baby that had been safe in her body just moments ago.

Suddenly, it cried, strong and wild. "It's a girl," the doctor said. "You have a daughter." And he put her on Elisa's chest. Spots of blood and white liquid covered the little body yet her skin the same tan color as her mother's. "Hey, baby." Elisa welcomed her sweetly. The newborn's eyes were closed and sweet little sucking noises melted Elisa's heart. The doctor cut the umbilical cord with scissors.

"Okay. I am going for a cigarette break. This morning is crazy already."

"Two more will be ready in a few minutes, sir." The doctor left the room.

One of the nurses grabbed Elisa's baby—too roughly Elisa thought— and took her to a warm water bath to rinse her. The other one brought a stretcher and put it next to the bed to take her to another room.

"Good job. You young ones usually deliver fast. I didn't even have time to ask you your name."

"Elisa."

"We're going to transfer you to the stretcher. It's going to be a little painful. So, here we go. Ready?"

Elisa nodded and closed her eyes. The two nurses grabbed her, one at the shoulders and the other at her feet. When they successfully transferred her to the stretcher, one nurse pushed her to the door.

"Wait, my baby!"

"It is okay, Elisa. We'll bring her to you when she is clean and wrapped up nice and cozy. Now, we need to hurry. There are a lot of pregnant women out there in the lobby, ready to deliver."

Elisa waited for her daughter in the maternity ward with six other ladies. They already had their babies and were breastfeeding them. Will I be able to breastfeed? Then she heard the door open and saw a nurse holding a swaddled infant. She felt her breasts swell with milk.

"I think that one is yours," said the lady lying on my right. She was the oldest one in the room, maybe about ... thirty.

"Elisa?" asked the nurse.

"Yes."

"Well, here is your girl. She looks hungry but you can't feed her too much at first, okay?" The nurse said. "Just about a teaspoon or so." She brought her to the bed. "Sit up and get comfortable."

Elisa slowly adjusted herself and removed her robe off her shoulder to expose her breast. The baby was wrapped with a soft white blanket with her small face like a moon. Elisa gently brought her out of the nurse's arms onto her chest. The little one's lips didn't know what to do. Her eyes were closed. Elisa stuck the tip of her index finger into the tiny mouth to open it up. "She's sucking my finger." She smiled in amazement.

Her neighbor on the left said. "Oh, she'll figure it out quickly. No worries."

Now with her mouth open and ready to drink, Elisa placed her nipple in between the tiny lips.

"Ouch!"

"It latched," the nurse said gently.

And then there was a sensation of release Elisa could feel from her breasts all the way down to her belly. The milk filled the infant's mouth as she sucked and swallowed.

Elisa touched her red cheeks with her thumb while she was feeding. She was so small and vulnerable. Elisa felt almost unbearable joy. "You are beautiful." One tear ran down from her tired eyes.

"That's enough for now, young lady." The nurse took her from me. "I'll bring her back after she poops for the first time, alright? And rest as much as you can ... you'll need it." The nurse left the room with the loveliest being Elisa had ever seen.

"So what's her name?" The woman on her right

asked.

"Her name is Lluvia, rain."

"Why Lluvia?"

"My water broke in the middle of the street and a few minutes after that it started raining, like it was clearing the way for her birth."

"That is a nice name for a nice story." Another lady across the room offered.

Elisa closed her heavy and swollen eyes. The voices and the cries from the mothers and babies in the ward faded slowly away.

Chapter 8
Mena's Construction

After two days in the hospital, Elisa was ready to go home. All six mothers left and a new set of moaning women in labor arrived.

"Is somebody picking you up today, Elisa?" a nurse asked.

"Yes, she'll be here after work."

"What's her name? I can put her on the chart."

"Juana Escalante ... but can I leave alone? I can walk out and ask for a taxi."

"It's again policy ... to protect the baby and you. You are taking medications that can affect your balance. Don't want to drop Lluvia, do we? Be patient ... this evening will be here before you know it."

Elisa nodded and held her infant closer, speaking silently to Lluvia. Of course I wouldn't want to harm you, my beloved. But I'm not dizzy or incapable at all.

The nurse smiled and left the room. Two of the laboring mothers cried out in pain and rolled on their sides to handle the contractions. The nurse poked her head in the door, but this was all normal to her. Elisa couldn't stand it. She wanted peace and quiet for her child ... and some good food for a change.

"I can't stay another minute here." Elisa muttered so only her daughter would hear. She made her plan as she was breastfeeding. When Lluvia was full, burped, and changed, Elisa put her baby on the bed and got up. She dressed quickly with clean clothes Juana had brought after the birth. Her breasts were full of milk and tender. She knew the nurses stopped at the room about every thirty minutes; she still had time. The situation made her feel like a prisoner trying to escape, or worse that she was kidnapping her own baby ... but that didn't stop her resolve. After she dressed, she picked up Lluvia then the bag of clothes and personal items. She scanned the room to see if she forgot anything. She gave a single nod. I'm leaving and I really hope I don't ever come back.

Because she walked calmly and normally, no one paid any attention. She was healthy, holding a clean, quiet, swaddled baby. Nothing out of the ordinary. At the Maternity Ward desk, families were lined up waiting to check out the babies and their mothers. Most of the women sat while fathers stood in line. There was a sign above the counter with instructions.

REQUIREMENTS FOR MATERNITY RELEASE:
- Release form filled by a nurse
- $2
- A family member or a friend to assist.

After reading the sign, she realized they were not going to let her check out alone. Elisa looked around, took a look at Lluvia who was peacefully asleep, and simply walked toward the hospital exit. Though her heart beat with anxiety — expecting someone to scream "Elisa Carama, stop! — she also knew she was the picture of confidence on the outside. Her only concern was that the nurse was right about her not being quite as strong as she thought. Her womb throbbed a little and she was lightheaded. Yet the breath she took outside the hospital and the warm sun on her face perked her up.

A yellow taxi drove in front of the hospital looking for a fare. When he saw her, he stuck his head out the window and called out, "Do you want a taxi?"

"Yes, thank you so much."

He ran around the car to open the door. "Let me grab your bag, missus." She handed it to him. "Cute baby."

Looking back at the front entrance of the hospital, she realized nobody had noticed her departure. She had escaped. The driver got in the car. "Where are we going?"

"Central Ave," she answered with delight.

When she walked into Juana's house, Elisa hoped her dear friend would be home, and she was, standing in the living room putting her purse across her shoulders. Her eyebrows raised in total surprise and made Elisa laugh.

"Elisa, what are you doing here?"

"I couldn't stand it any longer so I left."

Juana looked like she wanted to scold her but just threw up her hands. "I asked for the rest of the day off to come and get you," she grumbled. "Never mind. Okay. Let me hold this sleeping beauty." She gently took Lluvia from Elisa's arms and stared at her with tenderness.

"It's good to be back."

"I bet! But you look tired."

"I am a little weaker than I expected."

"Why don't you go and rest in your bedroom. I'll take care of Lluvia. I'll wake you up and put her down next to you when she's hungry. I'll be Nurse Juana."

"Okay. I'll be in my room." Elisa got slowly up off the sofa and headed down the hall.

"Elisa ..."

She looked back at Juana holding and rocking Lluvia. "You did good, hon. You did good."

The young mother nodded, too weary to smile.

Elisa came out of a deep sleep and heard Lluvia crying loudly. Her first reaction was to put the pillow over her head. She did not want Juana to come into the room, but the door opened slowly.

"Elisa, the baby is hungry."

"Oh, okay, I guess." She was not enthusiastic, but she sat up and held Lluvia for nursing. The infant found her nipple and settled in for her meal.

"Elisa, babies wake up many times at night to be fed or changed," Juana explained. "You'll just have to expect to be exhausted for ... quite a while."

"I can't breast feed her when I am at work. I'll have to switch her to the bottle."

"I can take her at night when she wakes up. Don't worry, I promised to help you, Elisa. We'll make a good plan."

"My future is so uncertain, Juana. I don't have

anything to offer my little girl." She felt so sad and began to cry.

"Don't cry, dear. We will all help you."

"I am taking Lluvia to Prudencia's." Elisa told Juana. "It's Sunday and the whole family gets together."

Juana stood ever ready to assist as she had been for these first two months. She plucked the baby off Elisa's hip. "You are getting chubby, cutie-pie. I mean Lluvia not you. Get your bag ready. You two will have a fine outing, a good change of pace."

Elisa frowned. She had hoped her body would return to normal quickly, but she remained rounder than she liked. "Yes, she's plump. Can I ask you a question?"

"Sure."

"How Roberto is doing? I notice that he's losing weight. I mean ... well, you don't have to tell me."

Juana stopped bouncing the chortling baby. "No, it's fine." Juana paused. Her face fell. "Truth is he's not doing well, then again the doctor said Roberto should be dead by now, but that's Roberto." She sat on the bed. "I don't want to even think about it," she sighed. "The doctor told him to stay home and rest but how can you tell a determined man not to go to work? He has to suffer this in his own way. I can only stand by and be there when he needs me. And he is happy to have the baby in the house." Elisa sat next to her and gave her a quiet hug. Lluvia started crying. "Oh, what's the matter now? Are you wet?" Juana got up. "I'll change her before you leave."

Elisa thought of Candelario for some reason. He hadn't even asked to see the baby. Nor would she offer to bring her to him. The contrast between the kindness of Roberto even when he was so sick and Candelario's disinterest was amazing to her.

"Okay, Juana. I'm ready. I'll ... we'll be home after dinner."

She handed Lluvia to Elisa. "Cover her with this

extra blanket." Juana put a pink blanket around and under her tiny back while the babe's mother held her. "That's it." Juana said. "That's better. Let me open the door, your hands are full."

Elisa almost cried at her gentleness when she was so heartbroken. She kissed Juana's cheek. "I'll see you later."

"Be safe. Come home soon, please." Juana closed the door behind her but Elisa felt Juana's deep loneliness all the way to Concepción.

When they arrived at Prudencia's, the twins were playing outside. One got a look at Elisa from afar. She couldn't tell which one he was. He ran to the house and came out with Prudencia.

"Elisa?!" she called out with delight. Was she surprised about Lluvia? Elisa had never said anything specific about the birth, but she had learned that in certain ways Panama City was small as a village. People knew people who knew people … and they gossiped.

"Where have you been?" She walked toward me to receive me with an embrace. "It has been so long without seeing you. I guess you didn't come alone this time."

She picked up Lluvia from me. "And how are you, beautiful?" She said with a baby tone.

"This is Lluvia ... my daughter."

"Now, I see why you didn't stop by. You've been busy." She laughed her most rowdy laugh.

"Hi, Elisa!" The twins hugged her.

"Be careful. Don't hurt her."

"Let's get you to the house and feed you some food. You are definitely losing weight."

"Well, I hope so!" Elisa grinned.

The family sat at the table eating soup and bread. Prudencia bounced Lluvia on her lap then looked slyly at Elisa. "How Candelario is taking it?"

"Taking what?"

"You know, having a new baby?"

I sipped the soup. "He hasn't seen the baby yet. His

wife Delila wanted me to let her know when the baby was born, so she could come and pick her up and take her to Candelario." I shook my head. "Isn't that nuts."

"Life can be nuts, darling." Prudencia agreed. "But he needs to meet his daughter."

"I know. I just have worries right now ... like finding a job. I was wondering if I could come and work with you again."

"I wish I could afford you again, but business has slowed down. There is a new fonda around the corner."

"When did they set it up?"

Prudencia sighed. "A lot's happened since the last time you were here. They opened about four months ago. I still have my old customers, but the new ones go back and forth."

"That's tough."

"I know. I know. I'll come up with a few new dishes and they'll come back. It just takes time. That's the downside of business. Anyway, I think you could work around here. There is a construction company that needs a secretary. The manager is one of my customers ... I'll talk to him."

"Thank you, Prudencia."

Lluvia fell asleep in Prudencia's arms. Elisa had noticed that everyone who held the little two-month old became softer. "Let me put this little one to bed."

Juana was outside waiting for Elisa on the street with an umbrella. The rain came down hard. She reached into the car for the child. "Let me get Lluvia." Elia could hardly hear what she said with the background noise of the rain and thunder. She paid the driver as Juana grabbed Lluvia with two hands and balanced the umbrella handle against her shoulder.

"Come on, Elisa. Quickly."

Water was already coming inside the house from the bottom of the door. They slogged in and began to mop it up with a couple of towels.

"You're home safe. That's what matters ... So, how did it go?"

"Well, she couldn't hire me again but there is a secretary position in a new construction company. She'll call me when she talks to the owner."

"Oh, that's a great news." Juana lifted Lluvia up so they were eye to eye. "Isn't that great, baby girl." Lluvia chortled.

"Okay, let's get out of these wet clothes. I'll make some coffee after that. Then, we can catch up with all the good news."

Elisa woke up every morning feeling low. She was running out of cash. She couldn't rely on Juana's kindness endlessly. This morning was no different, but she got up for coffee and heard the telephone ring. Juana must have been in her room. She put Lluvia down on the floor near the phone. "Stay here for a moment." She put a pillow behind her and gave her a rubber toy that she put straight in her teething mouth. It stopped her from biting everything or crying from irritation. Elisa grabbed the receiver. "Hello?"

"Hi Elisa. This is Prudencia. I have news for you. Finally, the Mena company is up and running. But they need someone right away. Can you start tomorrow?"

"Yes, I can! Wait, does he know my age and ... the rest?"

"He knows everything. Just get here tomorrow on time, okay."

"Alright, I'll be there at eight in the morning."

"Sounds good," said Prudencia. "See you then."

Elisa was so excited. She couldn't wait to tell Juana about it. She cleaned up the house, fed Lluvia, and got her clothes ready for the next day. The day passed more quickly when she had a purpose. Then she was struck by an obvious reality. Who was going to take care of Lluvia?

"Juanita, I have good news!" She wanted to be

exuberant about it for her friend yet Juana looked so pale.

"Oh, I am glad," she said with an unbearably sad voice.

"What is it?"

"Roberto was hospitalized." She slumped on the sofa. "He is not looking good, Elisa.

"What did the doctor say?"

"That he might not last a week,"

"I am so sorry, Juana."

"I've been preparing for this outcome ... just not in my heart. I ... I ..."

"Come, I'll make you some tea. Here hold our girl." That always cheered Juana up.

Juana followed Elisa to the kitchen carrying the baby with the rubber toy in her fists and mouth. "What's the good news?"

Elisa thought, Juana always bounces back so quickly from her sorrow. And she always expresses more concern for others than herself. "I found a job." She filled the tea pot at the sink. "I'd start tomorrow."

"That's wonderful, Elisa."

"I'm glad. The new construction company will hire me if I have a good interview. I have to be there at eight in the morning."

"Who is going to watch Lluvia?"

Elisa paused and answered softly, "I don't know yet."

"I'm off tomorrow. You go check out this new job. Then we can figure out how to find a babysitter for our Lluvia. I just can't make any promises right now. I have to be there for Roberto."

It was mystifying to Elisa how Juana always rose to her needs, even in her state of sorrow now. Elisa had no choice to but to accept the offer and hope she could someday repay the countless kindnesses.

The next morning Elisa arrived at Prudencia's house before they had finished breakfast. "You're early. It's only six thirty."

"I know, I was afraid I'd miss the seven o'clock bus.

Things always come up with a baby."

"Did you have breakfast?"

"No, I didn't have the time."

"Okay. Let me make some more coffee. There are chicken empanadas on the table."

Elisa looked around Prudencia's house. It brought back so many memories. From a simpler time, when she had just arrived from Setegantí. With so many dreams. She sat with a thump and put her head in hands remembering the whole course of change. I brought my whole heart to Panama City. Now, those dreams have turned into burdens. I hate you, Candelario.

"Here, Elisa." Prudencia interrupted her thoughts. She put a cup of coffee in front of her and added two spoons of sugar. "I still remember how you like your coffee. Even if you feel overwhelmed, at least you can enjoy your sweets."

Prudencia knew her so well. "Where are the twins?"

"Well, they're on the way to school now. It's nice when the house is silent. I took my day off, too, so I could take you to see Ricardo Mena, the manager of the construction company." She put an empanada on a plate for Elisa and one for herself. "I deserve a day off anyways. Mondays are slow. Plus, we can catch up. I am glad you got here early." Prudencia took a big bite. Through her muffled mouthful she asked, "So what happened to Candelario?"

Elisa grimaced. "He turned out to be a liar and a coward. He confessed everything to his wife then she came to tell me never to see him ever again. The nerve! He didn't have the courage to face me when I got pregnant or come to see the baby."

"Does he know that the baby is born?"

"You knew way over here! Of course, he knows—unless the engineer is horrible at doing arithmetic."

Prudencia laughed. "Forget about him. You know, you're not the first or last woman raising her kid as a single mom."

"I am so overwhelmed, Prudencia. I find myself crying for no reason. I have no aspirations. Even though Juana is so kind, some days I just feel like … killing myself."

"Listen to me, Elisa," she stared at me with her sharp brown eyes. "Take those thoughts and throw them in the garbage." She shook her head. "Don't let those feelings creep up on you. You are a strong young lady. You will survive this. For your daughter." She clapped her hands once and jumped up from the chair. "Now, let's go. It's almost seven thirty. This is your opportunity that could make everything work out."

Prudencia walked into the old building with Elisa following her from behind. She carried a bag of hojaldas and whispered to Elisa, "He loves them. I have to keep him as a regular."

"Good morning." A construction worker said tipping his hardhat as he exited while they entered.

"Good morning," they answered. "Come on, come on, Elisa," said Prudencia. "Watch your step. Wow. It's dark in here." There were no windows. The only light was a line under a door ahead. Elisa tripped on a brick in the middle of the hall. She grabbed Prudencia's shoulder to lead her.

Prudencia stopped at the door with the light inside. "Here we are." She knocked. The sound echoed down the hall.

"Come on in," they heard the loud male voice order. Prudencia opened the door. A bright ray of sun shone in from a field; there was no back wall in the office. They each blinked and squinted until their eyes adjusted. A black man with a hardhat got up from his desk. "Good morning, ladies." He walked toward them with his hand outstretched. "Hello, Prudencia." He shook her hand, looked at Elisa, and removed his hat. "You must be Elisa."

"Yes, I am." She shook his hand, trying to exude as

much confidence and competence as she could muster.

"Come on in. Have a seat please. This is my temporary office."

"For you, Ricardo." Prudencia handed him the bag. He looked inside; his eyes lit up. He laughed heartily as he took a big bite. "Ummm. Now I know you're trying to bribe me to hire your friend."

Prudencia grinned. "Oh no, hiring her will be the second good thing I've brought you today."

Elisa looked around. The small room was half built and had no roof. Fortunately, it was protected by an extended roof of the old building. There were cement blocks and bags spread all over the floor.

"Well, let's get to know each other, eh, Elisa? Let me introduce myself and the company Basically, I am the operational manager and owner of Mena Construction Company ... We buy old buildings, rebuild them, and then sell them for a higher price."

"I've noticed a lot of old falling-down houses in good neighborhoods in Panama City."

"Exactly. As you can see," Ricardo waved his hand toward overflowing boxes and stacks of folders, I am not the tidiest businessman. I need a secretary to organize the paper work, make sure that the material orders are placed and received on time, time cards put in order for payday ... umm ... and answer the phone, follow up on our leads about new potential projects."

"I did a lot of that at my last job as a seamstress's assistant and before that I worked for Prudencia."

Prudencia added, "She kept hungry dogs like you fed at PRUDENCIA'S ... and that was right after she arrived in the city for the first time."

"Where did you come from?"

Elisa surprised herself by answering with pride in her voice. "I came from a village near La Palma."

Ricardo gazed at her for a moment. "You come from humble origins it seems. Do you think you can understand what a construction company needs?"

"Yes, I can. Does it really matter if a business deals in bags of flour and sugar, sewing thread and fabric, or bricks and boards. What arrives in one form goes out in another."

His gaze turned to a stare and then he broke into a huge happy laugh. "Prudencia, I like this girl already."

"I told you, my friend."

"Alright, so ... for now this is going to be your place of work. It is not that comfortable, and I am sorry about that. We'll get a roof over it in a couple of weeks. Next time be sure to bring a shawl to keep warm."

Prudencia stood up. "I will let you two get acquainted and established. Elisa, I'll bring you lunch later. I have my day off and I'm going shopping!"

"I'll walk you out, Prudencia. This place is a mess. I don't want you to get hurt."

"Oh, I understand. We've had to renovate PRUDENCIA'S twice because of storms."

They closed the door behind them. Elisa stood up and looked around. She had a moment of missing Lluvia and her breasts hurt at the thought. Since this would be their livelihood, she just wanted to get started. "Okay, Elisa, it is time to clean up."

Ricardo left with some crew members to work on the new building expansion. Within two hours she had swept the floor, straightened up the boxes and put them in some semblance of order, and finally stacked all the blocks in one corner. She was brushing back her loose hair and a few beads of sweat when Prudencia came back.

"Are you alone?"

"Come on in. Lunch already?!"

"Yes, I got us some chicken soup and rice. Let's eat."

Elisa glanced at her hands. "I need to wash. He said there is a bathroom at the end of the hall."

"Go ahead. I'll get everything ready."

When Elisa came back she groaned. "That was disgusting. Tomorrow I'm bringing soap and towels and candles.”

Prudencia chuckled at Elisa's indignance. “They're all men here.”

“Roberto and your man don't live like that.”

“It's because they do what their wives say or catch hell. You just have to adjust here and be the 'wife' of the office. Let's eat. You must be starving.”

That night back at Juana's Elisa slouched on the sofa. “My back hurts. My legs, my feet, everything hurts. I'm not just an office girl; they had me help unload wood from trucks.” That was her first answer to Juana's question about the job.

Juana massaged her feet. “I know, Elisa. Construction is a hard business. It is hard for even a man ... but your body will build strength, hon. This is how it'll be until you find something better, okay?”

“Oh well, the pay is good.” Elisa looked at Lluvia in her playpen sucking her fingers so peacefully. She wanted to hold her but for the moment couldn't even move. “How was your day with the baby?”

“It has been a long day for both of us. I have to tell you something,” Juana warned me. “But please don't get mad.”

“I don't think I have that kind of energy.” I smiled. “What happened, Juana?”

“I needed a time alone to visit Roberto at the hospital. I couldn't take Lluvia with me. They don't allow kids in the hospital rooms. So I took Lluvia to Candelario's house. She spent the afternoon with Candelario's family.”

Elisa sat in silence. Finally she breathed out in resignation. “It needed to happen eventually. It was only a matter of time.” She looked at her daughter again. She seemed healthy and happy. “How did it go?”

“I called them in desperation and he said he would be happy to meet Lluvia. Delila was okay about it, too. I told them about you starting a new job. Delila asked about who'd watch the baby while you were working. I told her that we didn't know yet and that today was my day off so I helped. Delila offered to watch her during the day, since she is a stay-home mom. I'm sorry I couldn't ask you about today. Of course, I told her I'd ask you before I said yes to regular babysitting."

"I'd rather have you care for her... just as a person I trust most. But ... beggars can't be choosers, can we?" Elisa paused to think it through. "Delila said she doesn't want to see me though. And I don't want to see Candelario. So, really, how is that going to work?"

"I can take Lluvia before I go to work and pick her up later. We'll see how scheduling fits around seeing Roberto in the hospital. He ... he hardly recognizes me now."

"Oh, Juana."

"I care for you, Elisa, and how I love this little Lluvia."

"Well, perhaps this new job is going to work for both of us. I can contribute to the expenses." They sat pondering the demands of life. Elisa yawned. Seeing her mother yawn, Lluvia yawned too. "I'm going to put her to bed now, and I'll go to bed after that, Juana. You sleep well, too."

"Good night, dear family," Juana whispered.

"Elisa."

Her eyes snapped open. Juana was dressed and ready to go to work. It took Elisa a couple of seconds to realize that she actually had slept on the sofa all night. "What time is it?"

"Six."

"Oh no. I am going to be late." Elisa ran to the shower.

"I am leaving with Lluvia. I'll see you later."

She didn't answer for some reason. Although Elisa loved her child, she felt emotionally and financially frantic every day. All she wanted was a hot shower and a paycheck. She heard the door close.

Within an hour Elisa sat at her desk. Finally, after two weeks of working and cleaning the office, she felt settled. The heat of the sun was warming up the morning. She fanned herself with an empty folder while stacking employee time cards for payroll. "Payday is tomorrow. Done with that job." Elisa said to herself. Ricardo would handle the cash payments.

The phone rang; Elisa answered with her new professional voice. "Thank you for calling Mena Construction. How can I help you?"

"Elisa, Roberto is ...."

She couldn't hear Juana clearly. She was crying.

"What? Juana, are you okay?"

"Roberto died this morning."

"I'm on my way. Stay home until I get there ... Oh, I am sorry, Juana."

Elisa picked up her purse and left the office. She saw a couple of workers walking down the new hall. "Where is Ricardo?"

"He's up there." One of them pointed at the roof. Her boss was standing on a flat piece of wood suspended by ropes hanging from the new beams."

"Mr. Mena, can I talk to you?" I yelled at him from below.

"Sure, Elisa. Give me a moment. I'll be right there."

He finished talking to the workers and came down by pulling ropes through a pulley. He landed with a thump. "What is it, Elisa?"

"It's an emergency and I need to go ... a death in the family. It happened this morning."

"I am so sorry to hear that."

"I already finished the timecards for payroll. Everything is on my desk."

"Don't worry. I'll take care of it," he said gently. "Go be with your family."

"Thank you, Mr. Mena."

"Do you need any money in advance?"

"No ... no. It's okay."

He reached into his wallet. "Here." He handed her ten balboas. "Take a cab. I know you travel by bus. It's on me today."

"Thank you. You are a kind man."

When Elisa arrived at Juana's she found her weeping on the sofa. Another woman was there, hugging her shoulder.

Elisa sat on the other side of her dear friend and gently asked, "Tell me about it?"

"Hi, I'm Petra, her co-worker. Juana got a call at work. The hospital said that Roberto passed away about 10 am." She got up from the sofa. "I've been working with Juana for over ten years. She's like my sister. Our boss said we should go together." Her black hand held mine softly. "You must be Elisa."

"Yes." I said gently, "I'm so sorry, Juana," she didn't stop crying, "but we are here for you. Whatever you need."

"You need to get Lluvia. I've got Candelario's house number written on a paper over there on the shelf."

"No worries, of course I'll go get her. I'll be back soon."

Elisa found the piece of paper with the address written on it. Of course, she didn't *want* to go to that house to see Candelario—even worse, his wife—but it was the least she could do for Juana and her own child.

She flagged a cab and asked him to wait for her. The entrance was similar to Marty's house, sleek and new. From the porch she heard laughter and a sense happiness behind that door —the opposite of Juana's house right now. Elisa felt so sad for her. The love of her life was gone ... just like that.

A blonde boy opened the door. He looked about three years old and didn't have a shirt on. He gave her a big smile. "Mommy, there's a lady at the door," he hollered.

Delila came out and her shocked mouth opened in a

perfect circle. "Put a shirt on, Beto." Delila said to her son.

"But I am going to take a bath."

"Not now, we have a visitor."

As Beto broke down in tears, she waved Elisa inside. They walked in to the living room where Candelario sat on the floor next to Lluvia. Elisa didn't even want to look at him, but he was right there holding their daughter.

Delila said gruffly, "Candelario, can I have Lluvia?"

He looked up at her tone and saw me standing next to his wife. He turned white.

"Please bathe Beto? He is crying for it."

Candelario didn't answer Delila. He got up holding Lluvia effortlessly. "Hi, Elisa. How have you been?"

"I'm good." she answered flatly and took Lluvia from his arms.

"Papa, I want to go to the warm water." Beto stood naked in the hall holding his rubber ducky.

"I'm coming, Beto." As he scooped up his three-year-old he added, "You take care of yourself, Elisa, okay?" He looked at Delila who was scowling and disappeared down the hall.

"Roberto died this morning. That's why I had to pick up Lluvia."

Delila gasped. "I am so sorry. We knew it would be soon but … please give Juana my love until I see her … another day."

Elisa appreciated her concern. "And I want to thank you for taking care of Lluvia. It's been a challenge … work and a baby … and Roberto." She felt it was all coming out garbled, but it was true.

"Of course. Lluvia is welcome here anytime. She is easy to love and take care of. You can bring her in the morning too, Elisa."

"Okay, I'll bring her tomorrow before work."

"I'll be here."

Elisa left the house with her child, relieved by the outcome. She had a place for Lluvia to stay safe. After all, those people were her family; Beto was her half-brother. She was glad she got to see Candelario. Even though she had been afraid, she discovered she didn't feel anything for him. It was a relief.

Chapter 9
The Give-away

Under a black umbrella at the funeral, rain dripping lightly in a circle around them, Elisa stood next to Juana while Petra held her and consoled her.

"I am going to miss you, Roberto," cried Juana softly.

Even though, she was in so much pain, she held herself with dignity. She wore an elegant black dress and threw the rose on the coffin with grace. The small group of Roberto's coworkers and friends each put a handful of dirt on the lid as it was lowered into the grave. Elisa and Petra stayed with Juana, still weeping, after the others left.

The rain stopped, and Elisa shook the water off the umbrella and closed it up.

"It's time to go, Juana," said Petra gently. "Everyone is gone and you need to rest."

Juana finally looked around and saw a new group of people waiting for the next burial nearby. All were dressed in black and many were crying. Juana nodded. "It's time for us to go, dear Roberto." The women walked out of the cemetery, shoes heavy with mud from the loose dirt around the grave.

They returned to the apartment with the black and white tiles and settled Juana on the sofa with a warm shawl. Elisa made them a pot of tea and poured some for Juana in her favorite yellow cup. Juana held it with two hands and sipped it thoughtfully.

Elisa put a hand around her friend's shoulders as she had done for her so many times. Juana looked at her and sighed. "I need to talk to you, Elisa."

"What is it?"

Petra brought a chair from the dining room and placed it across from the sofa.

"Elisa, I can't afford to live here alone. I don't have Roberto with me anymore. We built so many memories together here at this house ..." She paused and looked around with wide, sad eyes. "I am sorry. I do love both Lluvia and you, but I can't stay here."

Elisa looked at her hands so they wouldn't see her fear. Although she understood Juana's decision, her world was collapsing.

"Petra has offered to let me live with her."

"Yes." Petra added softly, "Free rent in a big house."

"No worries, Juana." Elisa straightened up. "That's perfect. You're going through a very hard time ... I do understand. Don't worry. I'll figure something out." Elisa's heart cried silently. What will I do?

"I can take care of Lluvia until you settle into a new place and your new job."

"That would be so helpful, Juana?" She held back the tears.

"With pleasure, of course. I love you both so much." The held each other's hands tightly.

"When are you moving out?"

"In a week."

Elisa suddenly realized the burden Juana was willingly taking on. "Will you bring Lluvia to your work?"

"I will take care of everything, hon ... no worries. I will bring her with me or, if I can't have her at my job, I'll find another way. She'll be fine. So will you, dear one."

Petra nodded. "Angels appear in mysterious ways."

At the office Elisa didn't talk about her personal issues with Mr. Mena or anyone. She didn't want to be judged. It wasn't anybody's business. Maybe, she didn't want anybody to feel pity. She was barely able to get through the day but in an odd way, basic paper work made her briefly forget her troubles.

In a moment of darkness when she was merely staring at the desk, Mr. Mena walked into the office with a new folder. "Hi, Elisa, more invoices for you to file when you have a chance.”

He handed them to her. She took them but avoided looking at his eyes, afraid to expose herself and end up having to explain things she did not want to reveal. “You don't have to do it right now. I know it’s about your lunch time.”

“Oh, no worries. I’ll do it right away.”

“Did you eat already?”

Lack of sleep made her tired and lethargic. She could barely remember if she had eaten.

“Elisa?”

“Oh, I’m sorry.” She shook my head. “No, I haven't, but I’m going to Prudencia's kiosko for lunch.”

“Come with me. I’ll give you a ride. The crew is going, too.”

“Okay.” She agreed reluctantly, thinking that the men would be too exuberant for her state of mind.

“Great, I’ll wait for you outside.”

After quickly laying out the folders on her desk in preparation for the afternoon’s tasks, she grabbed her purse, closed the office door, and walked out to the parking area. Mr. Mena waved her into the black van with a warm smile. She got in the front and closed the door softly.

He laughed. “This is a truck, Elisa. Don't be afraid to smack that door.”

The three workers sat in the back, talking and joking.

Mr. Mena noticed that she was gazing quietly out the window. “Are you okay, Elisa? You know that if you need anything you just have to ask, right?”

She nodded. “Thank you. I’m just thinking about the filing.”

He looked at her gently. “Okay.” Then one of the men asked him a question about the roofing and they talked construction the rest of the way.

Elisa stared out the window again feeling nervous about seeing Prudencia, embarrassed to tell anyone, even her, about needing to let Juana care for Lluvia until she got resettled.

Mr. Mena parked in front of Prudencia's. As she opened the door, he touched her arm. "Elisa, tell Prudencia to add you to my tab from now on. I want to take care of you, Elisa ... I mean your lunch." He fixed his hat nervously.

She smiled. That was so sweet of him. "I have a tab with her already, but thank you for the offer."

Prudencia came out the door and opened her arms wide. Elisa couldn't help but weep a little as they hugged.

"What's the matter, hon," Prudencia asked with a tender voice. She gazed at Elisa's face a minute. "Come on. Let's go inside. Take the table in the corner near the kitchen." She removed her apron as she walked her in and sat across from her. "So what happened?"

Elisa began to tremble. "Juana can't afford her apartment now that Roberto's gone. I can't take care of Lluvia. Juana is going to take care of her in her new place for now. But I ..."

"Jorge," Prudencia called to her new helper. "Bring us some soup." She whispered to Elisa, "I have to tell him how to do everything three times. Not the brightest light." Prudencia always knew when to be matter of fact. It was calming. "Okay. Tell me more."

Elisa wiped her face and took a deep breath. "Well, I don't know what do to, Prudencia. In couple of days, I'll have no place to stay."

Prudencia leaned forward. "If letting someone else take care of Lluvia for a while is best for you, then do it. Juana seems to be a genuinely nice lady from what you've told me. I'd say you're doing the right thing. Lluvia will be cared for and loved." She stared at Elisa then continued. "Dear, I have noticed some changes in you. I see you are a completely different person since you had Lluvia."

"In what way?"

"For instance, you don't smile. At least, I haven't seen

you smile since you've had your child. She isn't bringing you joy." She sighed. "Hon, I'm talking to you as a woman ... as a friend … who knows how overwhelming it can be."

"It's a darkness I can't always make go away."

"I understand but don't add more guilt to it. You're not responsible for this change. You simply can't give Lluvia what you don't have right now. I know it feels dark and lonely. But you can reestablish yourself again. Juana is that angel that God sent you to help you out in this hardship."

"That's what Petra said."

"Elisa, do what your heart tells you to do for that little girl, *and* you know that you have a place to stay while you work it out. My home is your home, Elisa."

Elisa started to protest but Prudencia held up her hand. "I'll get one of the twin's beds ready for you tonight. You tell Prudencia you'll be moving on Saturday. Then she'll be able to care for Lluvia over the weekend." She pointed a firm finger at Elisa. "But you must promise me you'll get some help for your darkness."

"I will. I promise."

"Now eat!"

Sitting in the hospital lobby waiting to see a psychologist, Elisa remembered with a weak smile how she had escaped unseen with Lluvia. She looked around the room remembering all her exams when she was pregnant. Six people waiting to be seen by psychologists were all in one area and they all looked very sad. One old man, sitting across from her was crying in pain. The sound of that pain was familiar to her; it was not physical pain but a pain that came from within, from the heart. He touched his white beard frequently and moved around the chair uncomfortably. His black knees were ashen as if he had been kneeling on white chalk all day.

"Mr. Connor?" A nurse called and scanned to find him.

"Yes, that's me." He followed her down the hall, almost running.

"Elisa?" Another voice called her.

Her heart drummed in her chest as she followed her nurse into an examining room and swayed a bit as she waited for instructions.

"Are you okay?"

"I feel dizzy right now."

"Have a seat please," she said. "Let me take your blood pressure and I'll have the doctor check on you quickly, okay? Did you eat already?"

"No, I haven't."

"Why not?"

"I'm anxious about my life. I can't eat feeling like this."

"I understand. Dr. Vergara will assist you promptly."

The nurse walked out of the room. A few minutes passed by when she saw a pale hand opening the door.

"May I come in?" A raspy male voice said before Elisa could see his face. He walked in with a warm smile. Elisa could see the deep honest wrinkles on the side of his eyes.

"Yes."

"I am Dr. Vergara." He shook her hand gently.

"Hi," she whispered.

He sat down on his desk opened a file that he'd brought with him.

"I was reading your chart before coming in. It looks like you just had a baby."

"Yes, her name is Lluvia. She's five months old now."

"Tell me a little bit about her. Does she look like you?"

"She looks like me."

"It must be a very pretty girl, then." Elisa blushed. "Is the papá part of this change in your life?"

She shook her head and didn't want to speak. The question made her heart feel heavier and tears fell down her cheeks. "I … It's just that … I'm sorry."

"Please don't be." He handed her a tissue from his desk. "Take your time, Elisa. No hurry. I see you came here from the Darién. That must have been a very different life."

. "Yes. Not so much work to make money." She wept softly again. "But I wanted to come here."

"It's okay to cry when we feel overwhelmed and bottled up with problems, Elisa." He watched her face. "Can you tell me a little about the relationship you have with Lluvia's father?"

"There is no relationship." She felt so uncomfortable with the question and resentment rushed over her. I don't know why Prudencia made me promise to come here. Probably to remind me of the failure I am and how worthless I feel. I might as well get it over with.

"I can't sleep at night." She blurted out her words. "I get up worried and anxious for no reason. I get scared of what's going to happen from one day to the next. I hate her father but I know I got into this mess myself … and gave up my dreams." Tears poured out faster. "I hate to feel like this. I feel guilty that I don't have anything to offer to Lluvia … and … and … sometimes I regret having her. Now a friend will have to care for her while I work and find a new place to live."

Dr. Vergara was listening but writing everything down. "Is she safe with this friend?"

Elisa nodded and whispered, "Very safe."

He sat quietly with her until she stopped sobbing.

"Elisa, what you need to understand is that it is completely normal to have these feelings as well as to be afraid of these feelings. What you are experiencing right now has a name. It is called Postpartum Depression, meaning feeling depressed after having a baby. Your body is going through so many changes, and when you add stress and uncertainty to that, you feel awful. But the good news is that it can be treated with the medicine.

"It's important that you understand this has nothing

to do with loving your child. I know you do! Of course, she wasn't part of your plans; you are young. But truth is, life throws us these challenges no matter what age we are." He handed her a slip of paper. "That's the prescription to start treating you. It helps your brain feel good even in these hard times. It will help you be able to talk about the problems and find solutions. Do you understand? You are not a failure." His understanding made her feel a little better. "Also, it's important for you to do a couple of other things to help yourself. After work, don't just sit in a chair. Please, eat regular meals, drink a lot of water, and exercise a little. Take a walk in your neighborhood before going to bed. You'll sleep better. All of that will help settle your mind. The other part is thinking of yourself positively." He paused. "Repeat this to me."

She swallowed and sat up. "Okay. After work, I need to eat, drink water, and take a walk."

"Good. Simple, isn't it. You know, Elisa, everyone is afraid of something. We all have to learn how to deal with our fears." He smiled, filled a cup with water, and opened a drawer. "Here is a sample. Take this tablet now then go pick up the prescription. Within a day or two you will really feel different. And I will see you next month."

Juana was selling almost all her things on the street because she wouldn't need them at Petra's. Elisa helped Petra carry the sofa to the street.

"This is a small sofa but it sure is heavy." Petra laughed. Petra laughed about a lot of things.

"Oof, I know." Elisa looked at Lluvia who was asleep on the floor with blankets all around her. She looked so peaceful facing up with her arms opened and relaxed by her side. The sound of the floor fan close to her kept her cool. Her short, curly, black hair was moving slightly with the breeze. She was wearing only a diaper. They dropped the sofa with a thud behind a table that held kitchen things. All of the items had small pieces of brown paper bag with a price stuck on it. Juana was doing the pricing. Petra and Elisa walked back to the living room.

"Well, I guess we're done," said Petra.

The house was empty except for the fan; there was nothing else to bring out. "Yes, let's go outside and help Juana sell while Lluvia is napping"

"Let's sell as much as we can. If not, then we finish tomorrow." Juana stood and greeted the first customer.

After six hours outside, it started getting really hot. Lluvia woke up and cried out for her bottle and some company. Elisa changed her and brought her outside to feed her under the roof of the porch. Juana joined her. "I think this is it. I am exhausted. We sold more than half of the items. I'm fine with that extra cash. I'll donate the rest to the church."

"Why don't you take it with you?"

"No room at Petra's. I mean, the house is big and it already has everything we need plus more."

"Yes, it is a big luxury house," said Petra. "I'm glad Juana is coming with me. We'll be family there."

"Lluvia's done so we can walk to the church and ask the priest to bring a truck for the rest of the furniture." Elisa sighed. I know that feeling of family. I'll miss it … but still get a little at Prudencia's. It wasn't the sort of thing she'd say to Juana. It might make her feel bad. She didn't feel so bad about it all anymore. Just like the doctor said.

That evening, Elisa put Lluvia's pajamas on her. She was smiling and tossing her teddy bear.

Even though, she took her depression medicine, Eliza still felt regret that she was giving away the baby and her future was uncertain. It was a loop that ran through her head. Dr. Vergara said to be positive, but she didn't know how long she'd be separated from her precious girl. The pain was indescribable, yet she knew it was best for her child … looping again. She picked Lluvia up from the blanket lying on the floor. "I am sorry, my beautiful Lluvia. You'll be better off with Juana ... at least for now." She carried her to the empty living room where Juana stood in the middle of the room. It was an empty forlorn scene, like her heart.

"Are you okay?"

Elisa swallowed her sobs and handed Lluvia to Juana. She touched the baby's cheek. "I'll come and visit you every weekend—you and Juana."

"You don't even have to wait for the weekend, you can come anytime." Juana tucked the child on her hip." The pair hugged Elisa until Lluvia squeaked. "Get established, Elisa. Heal ... Take your time."

Elisa turned and left the house without looking back.

Chapter 10
Mamita Juana

Lluvia watched Elisa leave. Her sweet smile disappeared from her face. Her little glossy pink lips pouted with sadness. Three hearts ached.

Juana enveloped the child in her arms. "It is okay, Lluvia, Mamá will be back to see you before you know it." Her little chubby arms wrapped around Juana's neck as her sweet other mama rubbed her back.

"Are you ready to go to our new place? You are going to like it, Lluvia, because there is plenty of room for you to wander."

"Is Lluvia asleep? I haven't heard her in a while." Petra pealed potatoes and carrots in the kitchen, getting food ready for their next event.

"Yes, she is."

"It's only eight thirty. That's early for her."

"She went to bed at seven tonight. She skipped her nap." Juana gave a tired smile. "She's happy. It's hard to believe two months have passed since Roberto died."

"Time heals, Juana."

"This is a big event, isn't it?"

"Our business owner, Mrs. Laura, is very active in lots of organizations in Panama City. That's how she gets the clients. Even though she has that bad hip she works hard. She'll be one of the guests, too."

"Will she come to the kitchen this time?"

"No, she's very respectful that way. She'll leave us alone do our work as usual."

"It'll be a long and busy day tomorrow, but we should finish prep by ten tonight."

"How many people are coming?"

"This one is for about twenty politicians and their wives ... more or less forty total. Don't ask me who their speaker is ... I don't even know. Politics, ay! I just hope we don't have to hear them go on."

"We'll be safe in the kitchen. What time they are coming?"

"About two tomorrow afternoon." Juana paused kneading the bread dough. "I'll take Lluvia to the park quickly about noon."

"After they settle in they'll have a meeting until dinner. Saturday will be the big luncheon."

"We'll have plenty of time to get everything ready." Petra nudged Juana's shoulder. "I sure am glad you keep track of the details. Mrs. Laura is glad I found you."

"And Julia and Tomás are coming to help us serve."

"Oh good, they're very professional although Tomás is a little new to the job." Juana suddenly leaned toward the counter and held her forehead. "Are you okay, Juana? You look pale."

"I feel dizzy. I'm not sure ..."

"Here, have a seat. You're not resting well enough." Petra frowned. "Look, I hate to say this but Lluvia is keeping you awake all night long and it's our busiest time of the year with the holidays. Christmas is here. We need to find ..."

"I know! I'm sorry. I'll be fine."

Petra sat across from Juana with her mouth set. "Has Elisa come to see Lluvia yet."

"No ... I haven't heard from her for two months."

Petra didn't need to say anything. Her disapproval was written on her face.

Juana put up her hand to halt the lecture she knew was coming. "You're right. You're right. I'll need help so ... I'll ask Candelario and Delila to watch Lluvia this weekend, and we can take care of the guests with no distraction."

"That is the best thing to do." Petra sounded relieved that Juana found a solution without defending Elisa. "Plus, Lluvia will be with her brother. You know, more playing than with us old grownups."

"I'll call them first thing in the morning." As if that decision was medicine, Juana stood up. "I feel better now. Let's finish the prep for tomorrow and head to bed for a good rest. It's going to be a crazy day tomorrow."

Friday morning greeted them with a steady drizzle of rain. Juana called the only ones she could turn to with confidence. They were family after all. "Good morning, Delila."

"Juana? Is everything okay?"

"Oh yes, but I need to ask for a favor."

"What's that?"

"Can you take care of Lluvia this weekend? We have a huge group coming in for an event and Lluvia needs someone to watch her while I am working. She's crawling *everywhere* now and would not be happy in a playpen all day."

"Of course," Delila answered without skipping a beat. "We'd love to see her. We've missed her."

"I really didn't know who else to ask."

"No problem. Bring her over and she'll be fine. Beto will love it."

Juana bundled Lluvia, who gurgled in delight about going on an outing. Juana nuzzled her, grateful that this child was so resilient, so naturally pleasant. With the bag of Lluvia's clothes, diapers, bottles, and a few toys, they walked down the dark street and flagged a cab. The driver was sullen, probably exhausted, too, she thought. After fifteen minutes of bouncing Lluvia to keep her entertained, she told the driver, "Turn right on this street … here, please. Go to number 611."

He gunned the car through a puddle then came to an abrupt halt. "Six-fifty, lady." he said slugging his coffee. He grabbed her money and drove away the second she closed the door, hitting more puddles as he raced down the street. "Okay, so it's early, five-thirty in the morning, but he didn't have to be *that* rude," she muttered to Lluvia who gurgled in agreement.

The streetlight wasn't working. Lluvia chuckled and waved her arm when a rooster crowed from a yard. Juana tucked Lluvia's arms and head into the blanket against the cold, walked up to the porch, knocked on the door, and waited.

Delila finally opened. She was in a robe, combing her short black hair with her fingers. "Come in, Juana. Wow, it's cold outside." Although she had clearly just jumped out of bed, Juana was grateful that Delila wasn't grumpy, too.

"Thank you again, Delila, and sorry for the short notice."

"Is that Lluvia's bag?"

Lluvia pushed away her covers and reached for Delila, who scooped her from Juana giving the baby a big kiss that made the little one laugh. They all entered the warm living room. With the little girl tucked her on her hip, Delila closed the door. "Juana, I wanted to ask. Is Elisa alright? I thought she took care of Lluvia on the weekends."

Juana hesitated to tell the truth but decided it was necessary given Delila's generosity. "To be honest, I haven't heard from her for about two months."

Delila scowled and sighed. "You go to work, Juana. Lluvia is in good hands."

"I really need begin the guandu stew. I'll be back for Lluvia Sunday night after we clean up, okay?"

"Yes, Juana. Sunday night is good." She grinned. "And if there is any leftover stew …"

"I'll make sure there is—just for you! Please call me if there are any problems."

"Of course!"

Juana kissed the baby on each cheek as Beto ran in the room to play with his half-sister.

The luncheon was underway in full force. "The appetizers are ready!" Petra pushed the platters across the counter. They had been preparing since before dawn, listening to cumbia, tamborito, and calypso music on the radio in the kitchen. It was playing on low volume not to disturb the clients but every once in a while, Petra stepped back from the counter and did some fancy dance steps that made Juana laugh.

Petra had placed red cocktail sauce in a crystal cup centered on a white plate for each table. Every shrimp on the plate was the same size and laid out in a star shape. Juana sliced the fresh crusty bread and put it in baskets. The kitchen was busy and loud. The servers picked up the dishes to place on every table.

"Okay, appetizers out."

"Let's work on the main course now. I'll serve the rice ... you do the stew, Petra." Juana pulled the stack of warming plates out of the oven. She packed rice in a small glass bowl and then turned it upside down on a white plate, giving it a perfect dome shape.

"They are going to love this rice with guandu. You always season it perfectly. Very Panamanian, like this cumbia!" She twirled in her apron.

Petra's praise as well as her dance made Juana chuckle. "Well, actually it is a Colombian dish, but food travels. I just hope it doesn't dance off the plate!"

Petra added a long lettuce leaf, poured a cup of the meat stew on top, and finally placed a thin fried plantain along the side.

The presentation had a simple elegance. They looked at each other with satisfaction and then did the same with twenty more plates, finishing just as the servers returned with the empty appetizer plates.

"Is the main dish ready?" Julia always liked to keep the meal flowing, which made her an excellent server.

"All set and waiting for you."

"Just breathe, Tomás." Juana said to the young server who looked a little overwhelmed at the counter covered in plates. "It will be done before you know it."

"I spilled water on a lady's hair," he said hiking his new black pants up.

"Oh no, did you destroy her hairdo?"

"No, the water bounced right back. Luckily, the lady's hair has a lot of spray on it." They all grinned at the image, making the young man feel better. Tomás straightened his white shirt and loaded his first set of main dishes on his tray. He walked back out to the dining room with renewed courage.

"Okay, let's get coffee and desert ready, Petra."

"I can't wait for them to try the tres leches; it is so good."

"Oh, and save the rest of that guandu for Delila. I don't know how I would have done this with the baby here. I'll take it to them when I pick up Lluvia tomorrow."

"And after we save a taste for Lluvia, we'll send those extra servings of tres leches, too."

By two o'clock, the helpers came in with trays of empty coffee cups. Petra and Juana sat in exhausted satisfaction eating their own servings of tres leches.

"We did so well. Honestly, you are the best servers I've ever hired."

"Thanks. What an event. There are only two guests left at a table, deep in conversation about men in the city council," said Tomás.

"That's the sign of a good meal … it creates friends of people who didn't know each other." Petra got up to finish the dishes. "We're almost done with the kitchen cleanup. Tomás, can you help us with the garbage and, Julia, can you bundle the tablecloths and put them in the laundry room before you go?"

Mrs. Laura came to the kitchen door. "Juana and Petra," she opened her arms wide, "it was a success. I'm so happy. Thank you all for your hard work. May I join you?"

"Of course. Another cup of coffee?"

"Absolutely!" She walked in with a lilting gait caused by her bad joints, sat at the table, and kicked her shoes off. There was a raging blister on her white toe. "I went around to every table to talk with guests. On my feet for almost the whole meal."

Petra set a nice tray with a cup of coffee, sugar bowl, and creamer in front of Laura. "It makes us happy that you are happy with our work. Did the meetings and speeches go well?"

"I am always happy with you and Petra. You are great companions to me in these events, Juana. It is so reassuring that every detail is elegantly presented and goes without a hitch." Laura drank her coffee in a few quick gulps. "Even your coffee is the best in the city. You know, I really think women run the world. The men pose like roosters, get the high positions like these guys who gave their flowery speeches here this weekend, but people like us do the important stuff: raise children, serve food, comfort the living and dying, plan the gatherings. You deserve the best." She paused in her surprising little speech and grinned. "Soooo, I want you guys to have the day off Monday. You can rally for next weekend on Tuesday."

Petra gave a little clap. "A day off. I like that!"

Mrs. Laura pulled her tired body out of the chair. "Alright, I am going to bed, ladies." She stretched and took a big breath. "I am probably getting too old for this."

"Where's your cane?"

"Somewhere at the courtyard," said Laura. "I'll find it later ... or tell Tomás to bring it in to me. I'll be at my casita next door ... off my feet."

After she left, Petra bounced out of her chair. "Okay, let's finish with this mess so we can do the same."

Sunday evening, Juana knocked on Delila's door, hearing a cry that made her heart flutter.

"Beto, open the door." Delila yelled from deep in the house.

The shirtless little boy threw the door open like he was a gust of wind. It looked like he'd been in the sun too long. Juana could see the shape of the V-neck shirt he'd worn, his face looked like a lobster, and his blonde spikey hair had sparkling highlights.

"Mamá, it's Juana." The little wind slammed the door behind her.

She patted his head. "Hi, how's the baby girl?"

"Lluvia is being crying and calling you all day."

Juana felt a rush of guilt and sadness. "Oh, that's too bad."

"Beto, stop worrying Juana." Delila walked out of the kitchen holding Lluvia.

Her little arms eagerly stretched towards Juana. "Hold on, I'll take you to your *mamita*."

The sound of that word made a smile spread across Juana's face. I am a mamita even if I couldn't have my own babies. Lluvia tossed herself from Delila's arms; her little arms wrapped tightly around Juana's neck. Juana rocked her gently. "Hi, *mi hija*. Okay, okay, baby. I am here." Lluvia immediately stopped crying and nuzzled into Juana's embrace. "Thank you so much, Delila." Juana handed her a container of guandu and another of tres leches. "Maybe you can have these for dinner so you don't have to cook."

"How wonderful. I've already got the rice on. Listen, don't worry about the crying. It's perfectly natural and she can get used to being taken care of by us if she comes regularly. Juana, I've been thinking a lot about this. If you want, I could take care of Lluvia while you work during the day … and on weekends … if you bring her here and pick her up. That's no a problem at all." Seeing Juana's look of amazement, Delila added, "I mean it."

Juana looked around at the household full of toys and the warm clutter of a place meant for children. It was a contrast to the tidy formality of the large but public house where she lived and worked. "Delila, that is an exceptional offer, I think it would truly be a good thing." She paused to think. "Most of us grew up with some kind of bigger family. Now we seem so separate and isolated. I often think about the small village where Elisa grew up where I imagine everyone looked out for each other, family or not. So, yes, I will bring her in the mornings to see how it works. Then there might be a Saturday when I can take your boy on an outing, too."

Delila stiffened at the sound of Elisa's name but nodded. "Yes, I can see how that smaller community would be good. But we can help each other that way here in the city, too. Lluvia will cry a little bit when you leave and then she'll be fine."

Juana's heart softened at her generosity, and she held the child even tighter.

"She'll get used to us, even love us."

"Is Candelario okay with Lluvia coming like that?"

"Yes, he is more than okay with Lluvia being here, of course ..." Delila's voice trailed off. "I guess I want the extra love in our home, too. You see Candelario is not well. He was diagnosed with cancer almost two years ago and now it has spread."

Juana gasped. "I am so sorry, Delila. I know what you guys are going through. My Roberto got sick and we fought the illness ... but ..." Juana decided not to share the rest since Delila probably already understood what the diagnosis meant for their men.

"I remember, Juana," said Delila. "Please come on in. He's in the living room."

Juana was shocked at the change in the robust young man. His face was lined and pale as a ghost. His hair was thin. The memory of Roberto's face during the final struggles raced through her mind. "Hi, Candelario. How are you coming along?"

"Not so well. I'm on harsh drugs ... experimental ...it's quite miserable. Sometimes I feel the treatment is worse than the disease."

"So sorry to hear that."

"I honestly don't want to do this any longer." Candelario dropped his head back on the sofa.

"I understand. Roberto felt the same way."

He looked at her directly. "So you know."

"Yes, and I'd be happy to talk to you any time."

Lluvia began squirming. It was time to take her home.

"I appreciate you, Juana, for taking care of Lluvia," said Candelario. "She's my child and I want to do right by her."

"Well, apparently we're raising this child together, Candelario. I will be praying for you. Delila, remember there will be times when I can take care of all the children, too." She looked down at Lluvia. "Are you ready to go home?" The baby gurgled. "I have the day off tomorrow. I'll bring her back Tuesday for a half day. Have a good night, everyone."

"Good night," said Candelario. "Perhaps you and I could talk a little while together on Tuesday."

"Off course. Please let me know if you need anything, Delila, okay?"

"I'll see you tomorrow, Lluvia." Lluvia's third mom blew the baby a kiss.

Chapter 11
Lluvia

The city family arrangement worked for five years, each helping the other every week. On days there were no events just prep, Petra gave Juana extra time to take the bus across town to Delila's neighborhood. Juana took care of the wild little Beto when Delila needed to care for Candelario or take him to the hospital. Much as he hated the treatments, Candelario rallied and went into remission. He even went back to work. Lluvia grew into a talkative, lively girl. It seemed like the family circle was medicine for all of them.

As Juana walked up the familiar street to Delila's house to pick up Lluvia on a late summer day, she counted her blessings. The image of Lluvia as a baby came to mind and she remembered telling her every day that she was "the most adorable child any one could wish to have." And so the child was the first consideration for every choice ... always. She often thought about Elisa who had never come back to see Lluvia. What a loss for the young woman not to know she gave birth to this special little human being. Of course, she was too young to really raise a child but to ignore her completely was incomprehensible to Juana. But *Mamita* wanted Elisa to come back so she could ask her to let her legally adopt Lluvia ... and she had to admit there was a part of her that had a deep fear. She paused and looked at the clear sky. She said honestly and quietly, "What if she wants her back someday? I would be devastated. No only losing my beloved Roberto—that still hurts after all these years— but Lluvia, too."

When she knocked on the door she heard the special music of Lluvia's voice. "Mamita is here!" Excited chubby feet hurried to open the door. That sound of Lluvia calling her name made working hard worth it. Mamita had Lluvia in her life.

"Hey, child, I missed you!" Juana swung her up and

kissed her loudly on each cheek. The girl's long black curly hair covered her face. Juana swept it aside looking for Delila. "Hi Delila, where are you?"

"In the kitchen. Coming!" She joined them in the living room where she had collected Lluvia's things in her special quilted bag. "I'm good. Lluvia hasn't taken a shower yet. She's been playing outside all day."

"I see that soft skin getting a richer color. Beautiful." She stroked the girl's cheek. "I'll bathe you when we get home. Petra's made us a delicious dinner of *arroz con coco* with chicken and a special dessert."

"What dessert, Mamita?"

"Want it be a surprise?"

Lluvia took Juana's face between her two hands. "No. Tell me now."

"Okay. It's *Bienmesabe*."

"Yay! Almond and honey pudding. My favorite! Let's go." Lluvia jiggled her legs in excitement.

Juana noticed her bare feet were covered with grime and put her down. "Get your shoes on, my baby. And you can tie them yourself." Juana watched her hurry to the bedroom and then gazed at Delila's face, recognizing the expression that meant she had something to talk about. "It'll take her a few minutes to tie those laces. What's on your mind?"

"You know me too well! Here goes: Juana, now that Lluvia is five years old, she needs to go to school. Any thoughts about that?"

"Yes, actually I have and was going to talk to you when I have one of those half-days later this week, but now is fine. I know that school starts in about five weeks."

"She can go with her brother to the school a few blocks away."

"Well, I was thinking about registering her at Santa Maria catholic school close to where I work. You know, so she doesn't have to make the long bus trip every morning."

Delila nodded. "That's probably better for her, though I will miss her like crazy."

"You know how much work I have on weekends. You'd still get that time … even overnights. Not to mention that it wouldn't hurt you a bit to have your days finally free of childcare."

Delila looked doubtful. "Maybe," she said quietly.

"I'll go over to Santa Maria tomorrow on my break."

Lluvia ran toward me wearing her dirty white sneakers.

"Let's go, Mamita."

"Okay, do you have everything in your bag?"

"Yes," she said. "But my neckless broke." She held it out with her little hand. It brought memories of Elisa giving that crucifix to Lluvia when she was a newborn baby.

"I am glad you didn't lose it. I'll take it to a shop to be fixed." Lluvia carefully placed the pendant in Juana's hand. "Do you know who gave you this crucifix? Do you remember?"

"Yes, you told me ... Elisa."

"Yes, your mama who gave birth to you."

"She is not my mamita," Lluvia said firmly. "You are ... Can we go now?"

"Of course." They walked outside into the warm late summer evening. "We'll see you tomorrow, Delila."

"Please let me know what you think of the catholic school."

"I will." Juana put Lluvia down to walk and held her hand. She waved back to Delila who was standing at the door looking a bit forlorn.

Two days later Juana walked in the large double doors of Santa Maria del Rosario holding Lluvia's hand. She had already checked it out herself and liked it, but it was important to see what Lluvia thought. In the wide-open corridor, two nuns walked in their direction.

"Hi, I am Sister Mel," the younger one said. "You

guys look like twins with the same dress. How nice. I love it."

"Thank you. I have a friend that makes our dresses to for Sunday mass at Santa Maria church across the Street."

Lluvia covered her face with my hand and hid her body behind me. The green pattern of her dress blended with mine.

"I don't want to be here." Lluvia began to whimper. "I don't want to go to this school. I want to go to Beto's school."

One of the nuns leaned toward Lluvia. "Is it my black hat and long white dress that you don't like?" She smiled when Lluvia nodded. "We nuns have to wear it around here. It is kind of easy to spot us," she said. "Do you want to come explore with me. I'll show you your classroom to see pictures done by children like you and books you get to read." She slid Lluvia's hand in hers before the child had a chance to protest. "I'll take her for a tour while Sister Gina talks to you about registration. We'll find you when we're done exploring."

Lluvia looked back at Juana with a concerned face. "You like to explore, Lluvia. I'll see you soon. Have fun."

Sister Gina took Juana's arm as if she, too, needed to be guided through the new school. "We can talk at my office. Follow me, please. So, tell me, what's your name?

"I am Juana Escalante," Juana said. "I came here, Sister Gina, because it is time for Lluvia to start school. I live near here and heard wonderful things about your program. Also, I am Catholic. I want Lluvia to know about God and be involved in church in a good way."

She pushed open a door that said *Admisiones Escolares*. It was a large room with a high ceiling and heavy wooden furniture. There were crucifixes and oil paintings on every wall, and a large statue of La Virgen on a pedestal. "Here we are. Have a seat." Sister gestured toward a black chair in front of a large desk. Juana could hear the echo of her steps resonate around the room. The tiles were clay red, matching the door frames.

"This is a nice office." She sat down. "I love the crosses and paintings."

Sister Gina sat across from her at the desk. "Thank you. Father Benedicto brought most of them from Spain last summer." She opened a folder and began to read Juana's application. "So, tell me, please, how old is your daughter?"

"Lluvia is four, almost five." I said. "She is not my daughter, I mean ... I love her like my own ... but legally, she is not my daughter."

The nun looked puzzled.

"Okay, let me explain." Juana chuckled nervously. "Lluvia has been with me since she was five months old. Her mother, Elisa, left her with me ... she was a fifteen-year-old single mother dealing with depression, and she couldn't take care of Lluvia at that time. I thought she would come to visit often but ... she never did. I work hard and share care with Lluvia's father's family. I confess, I didn't track down Elisa. Time just passed so fast."

The nun frowned. "I understand, but it is a tricky situation." She put her elbows on the desk and rested her chin on folded hands. "Do you at least have her birth certificate?"

"Yes, yes, I do." Juana took it out of my purse and handled it to her.

"Is the father's name on the birth certificate?"

"Yes, but they weren't married."

Sister Gina gave her head a little shake of disapproval. "Okay, this is what we're going to do. Since school starts in a few weeks, I first need you to try to contact Lluvia's biological mother to give you the consent to be Lluvia's guardian or sign the application herself. The child can come to this school, gladly, but we need one of those documents from you as soon as possible. Otherwise, please get the father to sign and get a copy of the birth certificate for our files. We need at least one of them to either be the formal applicant or make you legal guardian. We don't want to reject your application."

"I understand and appreciate your help." Juana did understand and had half expected something like this. "I will try to find Elisa." She thought of Prudencia, whom she had met once or twice.

Lluvia entered the room in the rush, Sister Mel behind her.

"Mamita, I like it here!"

"Good! I guess we have to buy you the uniform, a leather book bag, and all the school supplies." Juana nodded at the sisters. "I'll be back to finish the paper work to register Lluvia."

"In that case we will be delighted to have Lluvia in our school."

Juana called Prudencia's kiosko. Elisa's friend answered the phone. "Hello, this is Juana Escalante. I don't know if you remember me …"

"I do. You are Lluvia's guardian. What can I help you with?"

"Well, Elisa never came back to see the child and she never made me a legal guardian. I am trying to enroll her in Santa Maria Catholic School now that the child is five. But they need Elisa to grant me legal guardianship for the application. Or sign the application herself. If not, I will have to ask Candelario to do it."

"Oh, she won't like that. Let me think a minute." While Prudencia thought about what to do, Juana could hear the chatter of the busy restaurant in the background. "I know she still doesn't want to see the child at this point in time … it causes her too much pain. She was in deep depression for a few years. We are all grateful you have cared for the child …"

"Along with Candelario's family." Juana added. "Elisa was young and irresponsible, but she's not a child anymore. She must be twenty by now." She began to feel angry at the excuses she was hearing about Lluvia's mother. Depressed or not, she could have at least asked about her own child. Selfish woman, Juana thought.

"Nonetheless, I think you should drop off both the guardianship papers and the school application, so she can decide what to do."

Mamita scowled into the phone. No doubt Elisa would take no responsibility. Still make the rest of them do the work.

"I'll have to take time off work to go back to the school to pick up the application and then to the City Clerk's office and then catch a cab to your place. I need them signed as soon as possible. School begins in four weeks."

"Yes, yes, I understand."

"In that case I'll drop them off on Wednesday and pick them up the day after."

"Well, I'll call you when Elisa gets around to it."

"No. If I go to all this trouble, it's the least she can do. Please encourage her to take at least that little bit of responsibility."

"I'll let you know." Prudencia's voice was cold and she abruptly hung up.

Prudencia called Juana three days after she dropped off the papers. "Elisa signed the application," was all she said. Juana caught a cab across town again and went into Prudencia's to pick up the papers. Prudencia had given them to her waiter and did not show her face.

It was a normal Saturday, the weekend before Lluvia would start school. Petra was putting the dishes away while Juana mopped the floor. The radio played a cumbia in the background and the phone rang right on the beat of a cymbal. Petra put the plates on the counter and answered the phone. "Hold on," she held the phone close to her chest. "Juana, it's for you. It's Delila ... I think she's crying," she whispered.

Juana dropped her mop and rushed to the phone. "Yes? Is something wrong with Lluvia?"

"Can you please come and pick up Lluvia?" sobbed Delila. "Candelario just died."

"Oh my gosh! Yes, I'll be right there!"

When she arrived at Delila's, the dear woman was curled up on her bed weeping. The children watched her with fear from the doorway.

"Beto and Lluvia, go play in the living room and close the door behind you, please." She sat on the bed next to her friend of many years. She understood her pain perfectly. "I'm here, Delila." And she rubbed her back gently.

"Oh, Juana, even though I've known this was coming for years ... not like this with no warning ... he collapsed at work. I am not prepared to be without him." Delila wept more loudly. "I feel so lonely."

She curled up facing the wall. Juana took a deep breath, knowing that she had to console Delila, also knowing nothing but time would help her grief. "Nobody is fully prepared for this, Delila. I know how you feel ... I went through the same pain when I lost Roberto."

"I don't know what I am going to do now," said Delila. "The funeral, the kids ...."

"I will help you with all that. I will ask for a couple of days off, so I can also take care of the kids." Juana kept her voice low and calm. "Delila, you'll get through this. I promise."

"I don't know. I don't know." Her sobs began to subside for the moment.

"Now, try to rest. Does Beto understand what's happened?"

Delila shook her head. "Not in so many words. But he noticed how Candelario became pale again. So suddenly." She moaned softly.

"Okay. I'll go explain it to him and be here with the kids. Just call if you need me. In a little while I'll bring you some tea." Delila nodded slightly.

"Thank you all for coming today to my husband's funeral." Delila paused. "He was a man who dedicated his life to his family ..." She caught her breath. "It is hard for me to be in front of this church without having Candelario next to me," she held her hand out to his black casket on her left, "except like this."

"He obviously didn't have much time to socialize as you can see around us... only you all: his sister Martina, co-workers, neighbors plus his kids. We were all he needed. You know he was a wonderful husband and father who fought so hard against his illness and survived longer than anyone thought ... for these children and for me. What a strong man." She cleared her throat, adjusted the mic with her hand, shook her head a little as if that was as much as she could say. "He is going to be missed by all of us. Thank you so much for being here."

The choir began a hymn. Delila came down from the altar to sit next to Juana and the children. Juana wrapped her arm over her friend's shoulder as the ceremony continued. She also touched Lluvia's hand. The child looked up at her with her big round brown eyes full of sadness. "I loved Papá."

"I know you did, dear girl." Juana helped the children understand the death but especially attended to Delila in the awful first few weeks after the loss of her beloved, thinking every day that she was a special woman. Despite Elisa and Candelario's brief relationship, she helped with Lluvia the moment the child needed her the most. She took Lluvia under her care as her own. Mamita vowed to help her without hesitation.

Juana leaned to Delila and whispered. "Bless you." She gave her a white handkerchief folded in a triangle. She wiped her own tears while the priest delivered his eulogy and completed the service. The small entourage followed the black hearse to the cemetery for the burial. Of course, it rained. This was Panama.

Everyone felt drained after the funeral. The children played quietly in the bedroom. Sitting on the sofa next to her friend, Juana asked, "Delila, I want to ask you something, if you feel ready." She nodded so Juana continued softly. "Now that Candelario is not here with you ... well, I know he was the provider. How are you going to sustain yourself and Beto? Will Marty help?"

She sighed. "I don't think so. She stopped communicating when we began taking care of Lluvia." She rolled her eyes. "Called her a child born in sin. How foolish. But I don't need her. The house is paid off already. My good friend Mary is the principal at Beto's school. She already offered me a job at the school as her assistance. People are so kind."

"That's wonderful, Delila. Yes, Petra came forward to help me. Everyone has had some tragedy, and they know it's best to help with the practical things."

"I'll be able to be with Beto and bring him home when the class is over. I can still care for Lluvia on the weekends."

"I want to help you, too. I can give you weekly ...."

"Nonsense. You don't need to give me anything. We're family. Just buy whatever Lluvia needs as usual. That's all."

"And I'll still help whenever I can." Delila looked away, too tired to continue with details. Juana stood up. "Unfortunately, I need to go to work. I'll take Lluvia with me. Please call me anytime. You know I understand."

Delila looked at her with clear eyes. "I do."

Chapter 12
Tattletale

Even though, we didn't talk about Elisa at my house, I still thought about her ... especially her cold voice at the end of the first meeting. School took my worries away. It was easy to understand what they wanted from me. I paid a lot of attention to my coloring, letters, and numbers, and played with three new friends at recess. I still preferred being at home with Beto but at least I had a little more fun each day.

In the middle of a chase game, the bell rang. "Children, bring your work papers to my desk, and I will correct them while you are in choir with Father," said Mrs. Gardinez after we got to the classroom.

I was still coloring my last farm animal, a smiley pig in the barn picture. There was no time to sharpen my pink colored pencil. I continued to use the pencil even though the point of it was flat. "I'm almost done," I whispered to Cindy, but she was already gone.

"Lluvia, bring your paper now, please," said Mrs. Gardinez.

I looked at the classroom. Everyone was in a straight line at the door already. I felt bad I hadn't finished but ran toward the desk, placed my work on a pile, and got myself in line where my friends were saving a spot for me.

"Lluvia, in here," they whispered. I felt like I belonged.

Sister Mel was waiting for us outside the classroom to take us to the little chapel at the other side of the building.

"Follow me, please," she said. Her face looked red in the heat and her chin looked kind of squished. I was glad I wore my white shirt with the soft round collar and thought I would not like to wear the nun's heavy dress all tight around the neck. Her index finger adjusted the collar and she let out a big breath. "Okay, put one finger on your mouth and point the other one at the ceiling," said Sister Mel while showing us how to be quiet for God. We followed her to the chapel in silence, except a few giggles in the back of the line.

We walked through the hall, passing a classroom where the bigger kids worked. Their faces were close to their books and they were very serious.

As we approached the chapel, I could hear kids singing.

"They started already," said Angelica.

"Shhh," hissed Sister Mel.

We entered the chapel. It looked dark and intimidating, almost like God himself might walk in at any moment. Now everyone was very quiet.

Sister Mel pointed and whispered, "Sit on these two benches. I'll be back for you in thirty minutes." She turned to wait beside the pew, pulling at her collar again.

With a flourish of his arm, Father Peter brought a stop to the last note. "Alright, I'm done with this group. Sister Mel, can you please take them back to their classroom?"

"As you wish, Father." The kids filed down the row between the benches. They were bigger and held their two hands behind their back. "Follow me, children."

"Now you little ones, come on up to the front. I won't bite," said Father.

We filed up into the front two benches. I was in the second row.

"Alright, I need a volunteer." Nobody raised a hand. "Okay, I'll pick a volunteer, then." He scanned the first row. Then, he stretched his neck to see the second row. "You, young lady, come here." The volunteer walked shyly to the front of the altar where he was sitting.

"I am so glad it's not me." I whispered to Katherine.

"What is your name?" He put his hand on her shoulder with a warm smile.

"Jazmín." She had a tiny voice.

He put his big fingers around her little chin and

tipped it up toward his face. "Jazmín is a beautiful name." He spread his legs, turned her to face the other children as he pulled her back close to him. "Can you sing any song you have learned?"

"Yes, *God is my light*."

"Great! Go ahead."

The sound of her voice was beautiful, bigger than her speaking voice. She had a great memory. Mrs. Gardinez had just taught us the song that morning, and I couldn't even remember the lyrics.

"Stop!" he said. "You have to be able to sing from your heart." He rubbed Jazmín's chest up and down. Her eyes opened wide with fear and she tried to move forward but his big hands held her close. I wasn't sure what he was doing but something about it looked very wrong. Maybe, the way he got that close to Jazmín ... so close that she was in-between his legs ... or maybe because he rubbed her little chest way too many times to make his point.

"You did a good job." He leaned over and kissed her cheeks. "Now go."

She walked toward her seat without looking up. Then he chose three more girls who, one at a time, had to do the same thing. Each time he pulled them close and rubbed their chests.

Finally, he stood and clapped his hands. "Alright, kids next Friday we will continue with songs until I hear each voice."

Sister Mel returned to escort us back to our classroom. Jazmín and the other three girls didn't say another word all day; the whole classroom was quiet for the first time.

I hoped the day would go by quickly. It was glad it was Friday since I could spend the weekend with my brother.

Sunday morning, I went to the church with Mamita, I tried to listen to the priest, but I never could get what he said. I liked the songs, though, and I looked forward to my ice cream after mass. I gazed at the priest and wondered if this one also liked to help girls sing from their heart. I shuddered and laid my head on Juana's lap. I enjoyed the little breeze on my face coming from the fan above us.

"Baby girl." I heard Mamita's voice calling me. I tried to cover my eyes with my hands but realized they were wrapped around Juana's shoulders and my head was leaning on her shoulder. I opened them slowly to find out we were outside the church.

"You're getting heavy, Lluvia," she said as she put me on the steps.

"I fell asleep?"

"Yes, you missed all the mass. Especially, the sermon from the priest."

"I'm glad."

She looked at me curiously. "Ready for ice cream?"

"Yes."

"Let's walk to the shop, then." She took my hand and, nodding goodbye to some friends, we headed toward my Sunday joy.

Yes, this was my idea of heaven: tasting the sweet flavor of the banana and the tart of the *maracuya*. That was just the right combination for me and the highlight of my weekend ... having ice cream with my favorite person in the world. I always smiled as I ate, getting ice cream all over my cheeks.

"Can I try your ice cream, Mamita?"

"Yes, lick here on the side."

I tasted but it was strange. I couldn't tell what it was. The color was a light brown and I couldn't imagine any fruit that color.

"What kind of ice cream did you get?"

"Coffee."

"It tastes okay, but I wouldn't pick that one. I like this one."

"Lluvia, can I tell you something? A little serious?"

"Yes," I agreed although I knew that question

always meant something serious.

"Elisa and I are going to court on Friday."

"What does that mean?"

"Well, it means they will decide which one of us will be your custodian ... your parent, your legal mom," she said. "Whoever wins will be the one to make all the decisions for you."

"Then you don't even need to go to quarter ..."

"Court," Mamita corrected.

"Because I pick you to be my mom." I said firmly.

"Well, there is more to it than that."

"Can I please go with you?" I asked. "I can tell them ... and I won't have to go to choir classes with Father Peter."

"Why don't you want to go to choir? I thought you liked to sing."

"I do but he touches the girls' chests to help them bring their voice from their heart." I said. "I am afraid he will pick me next time."

"Does anyone know about this?"

"Well the kids do, but everyone is afraid that they will get punished if they say anything about him."

"Hmmm ..."

"And ... they feed us *chiguagas* for lunch." I added to help her make the decision.

Juana grinned. "Oh really. There are a lot of those little dogs in the streets. They must cook a lot of them to feed so many children."

"Oh yes, they do."

"Alright then, I will take you with me on Friday. I also will go to the school tomorrow to talk to Sister Mel about this choir class, okay?"

"Thank you, Mamita." I took a bite of my banana ice cream. "Do you think they make chiguagas ice cream?"

"Only for the queen."

On Monday morning I worked hard on my letters in alphabetic order. The classroom was quiet. It was always hard for me to come back to school after a weekend with my family. We had taken a picnic to the beach on Saturday and had ice cream on Sunday.

Mrs. Gardinez was walking in between the rows. I heard her red high heels click on the white tiles. "Good job, Lluvia," she said. "Just work a little more on your lower-case *g* ... here," she held my pencil to trace the letter and show me how it was supposed to look. "See, make this line of the *g* longer so it doesn't look like an eight." She put the pencil down and smiled. I could tell she liked being a teacher.

"Thank you, Mrs. Gardinez."

Sister Mel showed up at the classroom door. "Good morning, children."

"Good morning, Sister Mel." We all answered.

"Mrs. Gardinez, can I have Lluvia for a moment? Father wants to talk to her."

The air went heavy and quiet. I could hear the echo of Sister Mel's voice.

"Sure," said Mrs. Gardinez. "Lluvia, go with Sister Mel. You can finish your work later."

"What did you do?" whispered Angelica.

"Nothing." But I thought about telling Mamita about the heart rubs. I walked outside to meet her. I felt every pair of eyes at the back of my head.

As we walked, the hall felt longer than before. Sister Mel didn't say a word to me until we got to Father's door.

"Okay?" She whispered. I nodded. She opened the door after knocking.

I had never been in this office. Even though the first day he kindly invited us to visit, I didn't think anyone had.

I saw him sitting at a large desk, and in front of him, Juana was sitting straight and proud.

She wore my favorite dress of hers. It was her other church dress, navy blue with full long sleeves and a white collar, and her salt and pepper hair was up in a bun held by a comb. She looked so pretty.

"Have a seat," said Father with a scowl.

For the first time I noticed he had big bags under his eyes. I was shaking. Mamita didn't say a word, but she looked at me in a way that was soft. She touched my hand when I sat. I saw a big picture of Father himself hanging on the wall right behind him. Like there were two of him to be scared of.

"Lluvia ..." He said my name with a long drawn out accusing voice. "You know that we punish lying in this school, don't you?" He paused a minute, but I couldn't say anything. I hadn't lied … tattled maybe, but it wasn't a lie. "Why did you tell your Mrs. Escalante about something strange in choir?"

I still did not know what to say. I shrunk my shoulders and looked down at the floor.

"Father," Juana interrupted, "with all due respect, Lluvia is not a liar."

"What are you saying, Mrs. Escalante? Are you questioning my behavior? Do you actually think …!" He got up from the chair and slapped the desk with his open hand. "I am the principal."

Sister Mel stared at him with wide open eyes.

He leaned toward me and stared. "So will you not confess your lie, child?"

I shook my head, just a little.

He sat back down on the chair, hard. "Well then, I was just going to suspend her if she confessed her sin, but under the circumstances … she is expelled from this school."

"No need for that ..." Juana got up now. "I do not doubt my child. I am transferring her to another school. Perhaps, Father, you should consider your own sin and confess." She took my hand. "Let's get your stuff ... we're going home."

I would miss Cindy and Angelica, but I skipped out of that school without looking back.

That afternoon, I ran through Delila's living room.

"Beto!" I hollered. "I am going to be in your school!" My brother was doing his homework but jumped up to greet me. "Let's go outside."

"Wait a minute …" I heard Mamita talking to Delila in the kitchen. "Shhh." I put my finger on my lips and put my ear against the kitchen wall to hear what they were saying without being noticed. Beto and I always did this. I whispered, "She's going to tell Delila what happened at the school." But they were talking about something else.

"Can you come with me to court?" Juana asked. "They want Lluvia to be there, too."

It wasn't about school at all!

"Of course," said Delila. "I just don't know why they want her there? She is so little."

"I know! It'll just be for a short time. So, while we're inside with the judge, could you watch Lluvia in the waiting room?"

Beto decided it was funny and giggled very loud. I pinned him against the wall. Even though he was two years older I was taller.

"Shush." I whispered ferociously.

He kept giggling and shouted out, "Mamá, Lluvia is listening to your conversation."

"Tattle tale!" I put my hand up to get him to stop. When I shoved my hand against his mouth I heard a thunk. It was his head hitting the wall.

"Ouch!" he cried out. I dropped my arm fast and stepped back.

Delila and Juana rushed out of the kitchen. "What happened?"

Oh no, something else I would have to be sorry about. "It was an accident." I ran to the sofa and put my head under a pillow. But I heard Beto say, "No, it's nothing. I just hit myself." Beto covered up for me. What a friend! I threw the pillow off and ran to hug him until he squirmed.

"Lluvia, sweetie, we need to go." Mamita said.

"We're going to bed early. It's been a hard day."

I looked at Beto. "Sorry," I mouthed.

My brother was rubbing his head, but he had a big grin on his face.

I had to wait for Mamita in the lobby on a wooden bench next to Delila. It was cold in the big building that seemed to be made of stone inside and out. I had worn my summer red dress and forgotten my jacket. At least, Mamita made me wear my tall white socks with my red shoes.

"Are you okay?" asked Delila.

I nodded. Delila fixed one of my two pony tails. She adjusted the red crystal ball ties. I touched them with my hand. There were big and smooth. I heard heels clicking toward us down the hall. I looked over my shoulder to see who it was.

"Lluvia?" a lady with a black suit and long skirt asked.

She extended her arms to grab my hand. "Come with me, hon. Juana is in the room waiting for you."

"Do I have to?"

"Go on, Lluvia," said Delila. "Mamita is there."

I held the lady's hand. Her nails were long and red; her skin was pale. I wondered how could she be so pale. She probably never left this cold building.

"I like your red shoes," she said nicely.

"Thank you. They match your nails."

She opened the door to a room with lines of wooden benches. A man with a black cape almost like a priest sat behind a large high desk. Juana had told me that this was a judge who would decide our family for us.

I saw Mamita standing up in front, holding her big hand bag very tight. Elisa was next to her, standing even taller with her high heels and her puffy hair done up.

"Mamita!" I ran toward Juana and wrapped myself around her legs. The woman they said was my real mother reached over to touch me. I flinched and shrank away from her hand.

The judge looked down at me with curiosity for a few

minutes. "Okay, I listened to both sides very carefully. Normally it is my preference to give custody to the birth mother even if she had to give up the child for a time due to extenuating circumstance. This, however, is an unusual case because the birth mother willingly gave up the child *and* made no effort to see her for five years. Mrs. Escalante not only voluntarily took on all financial responsibility, but the child clearly has deep attachment to her. While I think it would be good for Mrs. Mena to begin to cultivate a relationship with the girl … to develop the child's trust that she will not abandon her again … I believe the best interest of the child is to remain with Mrs. Escalante," he said closing a folder with a slap. "Juana Escalante is granted full legal custody of Lluvia Carama." The judge hit the desk with a big wooden hammer.

Juana picked me up with joy written all over her face. "God is good."

I leapt up and wrapped my legs around her hips. I didn't understand what the judge said but by seeing at her happiness, I knew we won.

"But … but I am Lluvia's mother!" cried Elisa.

"Mrs. Mena, I suggest you petition the court for visitation rights but otherwise, this case is closed," the judge said firmly.

I held Juana's neck while looking at Elisa standing there looking so sad. Her nice husband was patting her shoulder. Everyone left the room.

Elisa and I locked eyes until Mamita took me into the hall to give Delila the good news.

Chapter 14
The Broken Crayon

Ricardo held the door open for her, his hand hovering over the doorknob. "Come on, Elisa." He took his hat off and fanned his face. "Let's get you inside the house."

She held her white clutch purse tightly against her chest, as though it were a lifeline, and stepped inside slowly. She could feel her heart sink to the bottom of her stomach, sore, bruised, and heavy over the humiliating and unjust situation from which she had just come. Her legs still shook, a metaphor for the trembling in her very soul from the judge's final decision. She started to cry, her hand leaping to her mouth to stifle the sob.

"Aw, it's okay, dear, let it out." He enveloped her in a big kind embrace, sweat dripping off his temple as she completely broke down in his arms. His broad hand brushed her hair gently out of her face, and it gave her some small comfort as she wept. "It's okay, it's okay."

"This is just … I just … Why am I in so much pain?" she asked in between sobs that wracked her entire body. "I wasn't expecting to come home without Lluvia." She sobbed. "I was so excited for my girl to have her own room. I spent months getting it ready. Months, Ricardo. I don't want to even go in there."

He patted her on the head and smoothed out her hair as he let her cry it out. When she started to calm down a little, he said, "Listen Lluvia … this battle is not over. Far from it. We'll just wait until next year when I have enough savings to get us a lawyer. In the meantime, we can petition for visitation, just like the judge said."

"No!" She pulled back. "Next year? That is too long. I don't want to wait that long. She is *my* daughter. I brought her into this world; I should be able to see her! This is insane! This is unfair!" She screamed out the last words.

"I get it, Elisa." Ricardo said quietly, "but the child has lived with …"

"You don't get it. Lluvia is growing … and so is her love for Juana." She paused to collect herself. She grabbed Ricardo's hand, abruptly with an iron grip. "I am going to need your help. I am going to take Lluvia away from here."

"What?" Ricardo stared in disbelief. He shook his hand away from her, roughly. She tried to grab it back, but he jerked away from her. "Elisa, that's illegal, it's kidnapping!"

She looked frantically around the room, up and down, hatching her plan, not hearing him. "We'll go home to Seteganti where we belong, in the Darien. I never should have left in the first place. You can come with me, and …"

Ricardo snapped. "Christ, Elisa, what is wrong with you? You are being so selfish. Did it ever once occur to you that maybe Lluvia is better off this way? The woman adores her."

"How could you possibly even think that?"

"And me, Elisa, I can't just go with you to the jungle. What would I do?"

"But if you come with us, you can become a trader, hunt, build, anything. Life there isn't so much about money."

"My business is here; my life is here," he said, gesturing around him. "Panama City is my home."

"Ricardo," she begged as she grabbed him by his sleeve, "we can build a life, a home, anywhere we want to, as long as we're together, and with Lluvia we can be a happy family."

This time, he carefully pried Elisa's fingers off his shirt sleeve, trying to swallow his horror at this Elisa born of tragedy. "Elisa, I love you. But I am not going to let you act foolishly. We will wait like I told you." Ricardo walked into the bedroom and closed the door. It wasn't a slam, but shutting her out communicated his anger.

The air in the room was heavy, and her heart sank even further. She stood anchored in place, tears streaking down her round cheeks. The humidity and heat were suddenly too much for her, and she set down the purse she had been holding so tightly on a small red desk that was supposed to be covered in pencil marks from Lluvia. A row of new crayons lay on top of a new coloring book. The sudden motion moved a white crayon. It fell on the tiny yellow chair and broke into two uneven pieces as it hit the ground. She turned on a fan and stood there a moment longer, letting its breeze fall upon her face and dry her tears. She stared blankly.

She turned toward the perfect red table with the tiny yellow chair by the broken crayon, and said, with not a hint of uncertainty in her voice, "I will get you back, my baby. No man, no law, and no Juana can stop me from carrying you in my arms once more. Nothing will stand in my way, and nothing will stop me from being your mother again."

With a firm nod, she stood up and walked over to the telephone. She picked up the receiver, pressed it to her ear, and dialed the number, listening as the dial rotated for every number. She waited for a voice.

It came.

"Hello?"

She slid the curtains open, letting the light in to shine on her face. She took a deep breath. "I need your help. Again."

"Of course."

We didn't go to church that Sunday. Instead, we were busy getting ready for Monday school.

"I am so excited! I am going to your school, Beto." My brother was on the floor playing with me. We were building little houses out of wooden blocks. Mamita and Delila were sitting on the sofa.

"Are you sure Lluvia can just show up at school, just like that?"

"This is public school, Juana." Delila said. "Plus, the principal is a friend of mine. I'll bring you the paper work after you pick her up tomorrow afternoon."

"I have to get the uniform today," said Mamita. "Are the uniform stores are opened today? I know that some are open on Sunday."

"Yes, they are," said Delila. "But you don't have to buy the shirts. I have a lot of shirts from last year. Beto, go and get me the blue container in your closet."

Beto always liked a job so he ran to his room, padding on the clay tile floor with his bare feet.

"You'll only have to buy her shoes and blue skirts for the uniform," added Delila.

"Here it is." Beto dropped the box with a thud in the middle of the living room.

Juana lifted a white shirt from the blue container. "Come, Lluvia. Let me see how it fits you,"

I stood close as she put the white shirt on me. I brushed the sleeves down my shoulders and noticed a red small tag. There was one on each side. "What's this?"

Mamita fingered it. "Oh, I never noticed these."

"They're called epaulets. It is part of the public-school uniform," said Delila.

"Very nice. I am going to the store now, so I can get the rest. Let's go, Lluvia."

"Mamita, can't I stay to play with Beto, please."

Juana looked at Delila who nodded. "Alright, I'll be

back in about two hours.”

“Okay ... and ... can I have twenty cents to buy cold oranges from the neighbors? They are so sweet and yummy.”

“Here. Get some for Beto, too. You can go after lunch.”

“Okay, Mamita.” I hugged her then ran back to play with the blocks.

After lunch Delila began peeling potatoes for a dinner soup. I wasn’t tired. I looked up from my coloring book. “Can Beto come with me to buy oranges?”

“He’s napping right now,” she said. “After he wakes up.”

I felt grumpy. I didn’t want to wait but I answered, “Okay.”

I left the kitchen and put my hand in my pocket to make sure that the coins were still there. I went to the bedroom corner where Delila usually put my flip flops. I put them on and walked out the door quickly, shutting it softly behind me. I’d be right back. She wouldn’t even know I left.”

I walked down the street toward the blue house where the lady sold oranges. I could taste the fruit in my mouth already. She kept them in a cooler and a cold orange always cooled me off in the hot afternoon. I began to skip.

“Lluvia!” someone called me. I stopped, thinking I’d been caught being naughty, leaving the house without permission. The voice was familiar, and it was coming from a red taxi parked right next to the sidewalk. There was a figure inside but I still couldn’t tell who it was. Then the door opened, and Elisa got out. My heart raced. I backed up.

“Where are you going?” Elisa asked nicely.

I pointed at the blue house. “To buy oranges.”

“It is hot out here. Let me give you a ride.” Her voice was kind.

I hesitated and thought of racing back up the street ... but then I thought I really want those oranges and, well, this ride might make it even quicker. Delila won't know I left the house. And I know this person so it wasn't not like driving away with a stranger. "Okay." I accepted, feeling unsure, but the oranges waited.

I got in the car. She held me close to her. I didn't like that. She didn't give any instruction to the driver. He just drove. He passed the blue house of the orange lady. I knew right then that I was in trouble. "Where are we going, Elisa?"

"Home," she said in a grown-up voice that always meant there was no argument. "The place I should not have left. It's where we belong."

I began to cry in silence. She was taking my world away. I would never see Mamita or Beto again. "I should have never got into this car," I whispered. I looked at Elisa's hands; they were shaking just like mine. How strange. Mamita would find me after she got home. I felt sure for a minute. I kept silent as the taxi drove on through the noisy streets of Panama City.

I heard a bus honk. I looked back and saw the Bus #32. It was a bus route Mamita and I had taken to go ... if only I could remember where.

"Thirty-two, thirty-two, thirty-two, I repeated in my head. Oh, that is the bus that goes back to Delila's street from some restaurants and shops.

We turned into an ally off that big street and the taxi stopped. Elisa handed him money. I still had the coins for oranges clutched in my sweaty palm. "Let's go, Lluvia." Elisa walked me toward the back of a restaurant. There were garbage cans full of old smelly food. She held my hand too tightly. I looked back and saw the taxi disappear into traffic at the corner just as another Bus #32 drove by.

"Elisa!" A short stocky lady opened the door. Elisa walked into the kitchen still pulling my hand.

"I made it, Prudencia."

Prudencia closed the door behind her. She led us up some stairs into a little office. Right away she closed the white curtains on the window overlooking the street. "Are you taking her to Darien?"

I sat down on an old ripped couch. "I heard about that place before. You take a boat to get there." I dug my finger into the yellow foam exposed on the sofa and grabbed the black spring that was sticking out of it too.

They looked at me in surprise, but Elisa answered, "Prudencia, I am going to El Muelle Fiscal to find out what time the next boat leaves for La Palma, probably tomorrow morning. Then I can catch a piragua to Chepigana … Maybe I can get a message to Jito to pick me up." She laughed in a hard way. "I remember when he told me 'The #12 bus. Remember that. It will bring you to the market at El Muelle Fiscal whenever you need to get there … if you ever need to come back to Seteganti.' At the time I thought Never!" Elisa paused, shook her head softly, and looked up at the ceiling. After a moment she asked, "Can you take care of Lluvia? I'll be back shortly."

I shredded a little piece of foam. I would never see Mamita if I got on a boat to La … La Palma ... then those other places.

"Go ahead. Please, don't take too long because I could really get in trouble. Did anyone see Lluvia get in the car with you?"

"No ... nobody."

Prudencia hugged her. "I hope you're able to take your daughter with you, Elisa. I know how much pain you're in right now. So, I will help you every way I can, but ..."

"She's my daughter, Prudencia. There is no law that can change that, and *nobody* is going to take her from me."

"Does Ricardo know about this?"

"No ... I'm leaving him … for now. He doesn't understand. This is how I must do it. I have no choice."

Elisa put her hand to her forehead and closed her eyes. "I've got to go now." Then she snapped open her eyes and grabbed my two hands.

"I'll be back in an hour, Lluvia," she said softly. "Prudencia will watch you for now. We are going to an amazing place, where I grew up. You will see amazing animals, beautiful flowers, and kind, kind people. You'll meet Ninfa, my aunt. She is just like Juana."

I looked down and did not respond. Nobody is like Mamita. She closed the door behind her.

"Everything is going to be okay, Lluvia," said Prudencia softly, but she had deep lines between her eyes.

I stood up and looked out the window. Elisa was standing outside on the street waiting for a taxi.

"Are you okay, hon?"

I had an idea. A trick Beto once played on me. "I'm thirsty. Can I have some water, please?"

"Sure. And I'll get you a fresh warm hojalda, too, with honey on it."

I followed her to the top of the stairs. This was my chance. When she went down and turned into the kitchen, I ran on tiptoes downstairs and rushed out the front door onto the sidewalk by the big street. I heard Prudencia called out. "Lluvia!" but she did not follow me as I ran toward the bus stop. She walked toward Elisa who was still standing on the corner trying to flag a taxi. I slowed down and hid between people walking down the street. "Please don't look back. Please don't look back," I prayed silently. The bus stop was the other direction from her. Elisa extended her arm. "Taxi!" she called so loud I could hear her, and one skidded to a stop at the curb in front of her. She got in before Prudencia got to her. The taxi faded into the traffic and I let out a breath.

I walked slowly to the bus stop winding in between tall people and I sat down beside a fat man so Prudencia wouldn't see me. A police officer in a blue uniform walked by. I got very nervous because I felt that I was doing something wrong by escaping my mother who was not my mother. I was afraid he would might take me back to the restaurant. A woman rolled a baby carriage up to the bus stop. The baby was crying so I got up, touched her cheek, and the baby stopped crying. The mom said, "Thank you, dear." I was being nice, but I also wanted the policeman to think this was my family.

Two buses passed by: #62 and #28. Not mine. Thirty-two, thirty-two, thirty-two.

I was scared that Prudencia or Elisa would show up while I was waiting. I thought about taking a taxi but I looked down at my palm still clutching the coins. Not enough orange money. Prudencia always paid with paper money when we took taxis. And someone would think it strange that a little girl was on the curb flagging a taxi without her parents.

Then far down the block, I saw Bus #32. The number was printed big on the windshield.

"Please hurry." I whispered and jiggled my flip flops nervously. I looked around for Prudencia or Elisa. Not there. The bus honked loud when it pulled up at the bus stop. I held out the coins to the driver. He took one and left the other. I clutched it and found a bench in the middle of the bus. My heart was thumping so fast. I looked out the window. Finally, there came Prudencia looking for me. She her shoulders slumped the way Beto did when he was hiding. Oh she doesn't want anyone to see her. That's why she didn't come out. She thinks she is doing something wrong. I ducked down on my seat until the bus pulled away.

Tears suddenly fell down my tired face. I was afraid someone would notice so I quickly wiped my eyes and pressed my nose on the window. It was getting dark already. Don't cry, Lluvia, I ordered myself. I looked straight through the front window of the bus. I could see the number thirty-two reversed from the inside.

The bus had many stops. I was looking for the store where Delila took us to get groceries. It was right beside a bus stop. I looked into the back of the bus. It was almost empty; I began to feel afraid again. What if it's not there? What if I get off at the wrong bus stop? I'll be lost with no money.

The bus slowed down. *Is that the right store?* I stood up by the window to look for more familiar signs.

"Stop!" yelled an old lady carrying groceries bags. She sat two rows in front of me. A celery stalk hung out from one of her bags. The bus stopped, the doors opened with a swoosh of air, and she got off. I felt the bus begin to move again. "Stop!" I yelled and ran toward the front. When he stopped, I almost fell over. "Well, are you going to get off or not?"

"Oh yes, thank you." And I leapt down the steps onto the curb. The feeling of being lost crept up on me again ... but I didn't hesitate. I walked back toward the store I saw earlier. I was sure they knew Delila ... They had to know her ... everyone knew her.

It was strange. While I was walking to the store, a soft breeze blew on my face and hair. The sun was down already, but I could see the most beautiful colors in the sky. They were almost like a painting in Petra's big house. The honking buses and cars were shrill. I walked to the store and stood in the middle of the entrance. There was a commotion inside the store. Two police officers stood at the counter taking notes, talking to a woman with her back to me. She had papers in her hand. Oh, but then she moved her hand in a special way as she was talking. I would recognize that sway of her fingers anywhere. She was upset. I did not want her to be upset. "Mamita!" I screamed from a very deep place in my chest ... that place that is mostly quiet, that place that only I could reach. I ran to her. Juana was the guardian of everything and I swore in my heart that I would forever guard her too. I would stay by her side no matter what, and never upset her again.

Juana turned around. "Lluvia!" She cried with joy, ran to me, and swooped me up. I wrapped my legs

around her waist and buried my head on her shoulder.
"I'm sorry, Mamita." I opened my hand. The last coin I
was holding, dropped, and clinked across the floor. I was
too tired to worry about that.

"You didn't do anything wrong, Lluvia. Mamita
loves you. Thank you for being brave and coming back
to me." Mamita stroked my head.

"She won't take me from you again, Mamita."

"Take you? Who? What do you mean?"

"Mrs. Escalante." The police officer came over to us.
"I have to ask Lluvia some questions. We want to make
sure this doesn't happen again. It won't take too long."

She looked at me. I nodded.

"Tell them what happened and then we'll go home so
I can make you something for dinner ... with oranges for
desert."

"Okay." I was limp and hungry, but I was with my
mother. That was all that mattered.

Chapter 16
Mercy

Juana sat next to me on the porch. "They put Elisa in a mental hospital for a month, but Ricardo got her out. She had to promise never to try to see you again or she would go to jail."

Mamita finished her story and I stopped swinging. I came out of my daze. I felt like I had been swept back into that time of my childhood. It was not so simple as I had imagined. Elisa was not such a villain.

There was Elisa's little daughter, standing next to my girl under the marañon tree. They were the same height, their dresses stained by the red cashew fruit.

"She looks like Ricardo more than Elisa."

"She got her daddy's skin color. She still has Elisa's smile."

Resentment rose again in my throat. I asked a question that was always in my heart. "There is one part I have so much trouble understanding. How could she give me away like a pair shoes and never get in touch?" I felt like a swirl of old wounds had been stirred with a wooden spoon. I touched the crucifix from Elisa that I still wore. Her only gift. The mix of emotions within my heart finally erupted through my eyes and I let it flow.

Juana snuggled closer. She held me from the side. She looked at my face with a smile and said, "As a child Elisa didn't have someone to love her the way I love you ... yet she was incredibly kind to me when my Roberto died. I dedicated my life to you and raised you with peace in my heart. When we don't know exactly why something happens in our life, I like to think of it as a gift. A drop of mercy from God. You were and are the daughter that I always wished for... you were a precious miracle in my life. A kind of gift from Elisa."

"How can I ever forgive her?"

"She tried the best she could. She deserves some mercy, too. She gave you the gift of me." Juana chuckled. "I never thought of it that way before. I forgave her and realized that forgiveness—mercy— is also a gift to oneself, Lluvia. She and Delila forgave Candelario and look how big a family we had. They gave you a brother, Beto. It was good for your heart. Now set yourself free. This return of Elisa in your life is good. You can be delivered from the resentment and pain of the memory that she lost you and you lost her because you've each had a life full of love."

I finally realized what Mamita, that incomparable woman, was saying. My anger was a prison. The whole picture of Elisa's early life, my early life, and Juana's dedication flashed before me like a beautiful work of art. So many women, including me, had created an extraordinary family line. I waved my hand for the two girls to join us on the porch.

"That's my baby girl." Mamita smiled. "That's it." She rubbed her gentle gnarled hand on my back.

I saw my daughter and my little sister come toward me laughing. It brought back memories of myself running with my little half-brother toward Juana when she picked us up from school. Delila putting me down for a nap. Petra feeding me tres leches, and more. Family was much rounder than I ever thought. It didn't need to be tied to the idea of one father or mother, loved and lost. I would open my heart to this new little girl in our lives … and our mother, Elisa.

I felt freedom flow through me with this sense of mercy. My world felt large and promising. I turned to Juana. "Maybe we should all go to Setegantí to meet Aunt Ninfa, Jito, and the sloths."

The End